The Grudge

by

Kathi Daley

This book is a work of fiction. Names, characters, places, and incidents either are products of the author's imagination or are used fictitiously. Any resemblance to actual events or locales or persons, living or dead, is entirely coincidental.

Thank you to Randy Ladenheim-Gil for the editing.

I want to thank the very talented Jessica Fischer for the cover art.

I so appreciate Bruce Curran, who is always ready and willing to answer my cyber questions.

And, of course, thanks to the readers and bloggers in my life, who make doing what I do possible.

And finally I want to thank my sister Christy for always lending an ear and my husband Ken for allowing me time to write by taking care of everything else.

Books by Kathi Daley

Come for the murder, stay
for the romance.

Zoe Donovan Cozy Mystery:
Halloween Hijinks
The Trouble With Turkeys
Christmas Crazy
Cupid's Curse
Big Bunny Bump-off
Beach Blanket Barbie
Maui Madness
Derby Divas
Haunted Hamlet
Turkeys, Tuxes, and Tabbies
Christmas Cozy
Alaskan Alliance
Matrimony Meltdown
Soul Surrender
Heavenly Honeymoon
Hopscotch Homicide
Ghostly Graveyard
Santa Sleuth
Shamrock Shenanigans – *January 2016*

Zimmerman Academy Shorts:
The New Normal – *January 2016*

Paradise Lake Cozy Mystery:

Pumpkins in Paradise
Snowmen in Paradise
Bikinis in Paradise
Christmas in Paradise
Puppies in Paradise
Halloween in Paradise

Whales and Tails Cozy Mystery:

Romeow and Juliet
The Mad Catter
Grimm's Furry Tail
Much Ado About Felines
The Legend of Tabby Hollow
Cat of Christmas Past
A Tale of Two Tabbies – *February 2016*

Seacliff High Mystery:

The Secret
The Curse
The Relic
The Conspiracy
The Grudge

Road to Christmas Romance:

Road to Christmas Past

Chapter 1

"I can't believe someone was murdered on our first day here." Alyson Prescott held the neck of her down jacket closed as the howling wind sent sheets of snow horizontally across the landscape. Just two hours ago she had arrived at this idyllic mountain resort, which was nestled into the foothills of the towering rocky peaks that made up the Canadian Rockies with her friends, Mackenzie Reynolds and Trevor Johnson. Devon Stevenson, her boyfriend of four months, and his brother, Eli, had been spending the Christmas holiday at the resort with their father, who had been hired to beef up resort security.

"I know," Mac yelled, so as to be heard over the sound of the blizzard that raged all around them. "Here I thought this trip was going to be about skiing and romantic nights with Eli. Instead I find myself in the middle of some Agatha Christie novel. Seriously, whoever said life isn't fair was dead accurate."

Part of a tree branch whizzed past Alyson's head. "Tell me about it. Devon's been promising me romantic sleigh rides under the stars, world-class dining, and the best skiing in North America. Instead I find myself in danger of being decapitated by the foliage."

"I hope this doesn't turn into one of those hugely complex and dangerous situations we seem to find ourselves in at every turn." Mac jumped when a clump of snow fell off a nearby tree. "'Cause really, I've had my monthly quota of dead bodies and people who want to kill me."

"I'm sure the local police will take care of things," Alyson consoled her best friend. "Don't worry; we'll be on the slopes first thing in the morning."

"Uh, have you noticed the blizzard we're standing in the middle of?" Mac hopped up and down in an effort to keep from getting frostbite.

"I guess it is a little windy," Alyson acknowledged.

"A little windy? You know I'm not a big fan of the cold, but a snowy week at a mountain resort is one thing; gale force wind and subzero temperatures are quite another."

"This?" Alyson asked. "This is nothing. I'm sure it'll blow over before the sun rises over the mountain."

"I hope so. I got new skis and a supercute ski outfit for this trip. I'd hate to have them go to waste. I wonder what's taking the guys so long."

Alyson shielded her eyes against the blinding weather as she tried to spot Trevor, Devon, and Eli in the crowd. They'd pushed themselves forward through the throngs of onlookers who had come out for the main event over twenty minutes ago. Apparently a dead body was big news at the isolated resort.

"I think I see them talking to resort security." Alyson pointed into the distance. "I hope they hurry. I'm starving. I haven't eaten all day."

"I know what you mean. I feel a little guilty for being so focused on my stomach when some guy just got his throat slit, but the food on the plane left a lot to be desired."

"You heard the guy's throat was slit?" Alyson blew into her glove-covered hands in an attempt to warm them.

"So far I've heard the guy died via a slit throat, a gunshot wound, and strangulation." Mac wrapped her arm through Alyson's and huddled close. "I don't think anyone really knows for sure yet. I guess we'll have to wait until the guys get back to find out."

"I hope they hurry. I can't feel my feet anymore," Alyson said. "I wonder what the temperature is."

"I heard someone say it was minus twenty Celsius," Mac yelled over the thunder of the wind. "I think we should go inside."

"I think I see them coming." Alyson waved at Devon through the crowd, although she doubted he saw her because he had his head down against the driving blizzard. Huge drifts were beginning to form as snow was shifted by the power of the wind.

"So what'd you find out?" Alyson shouted when he finally made his way over to where she was waiting with Mac.

"Let's get inside and I'll tell you." Devon took Alyson by her gloved hand and led her down the road toward Rosa's Mexican Cantina.

The restaurant was decorated in a traditional Mexican motif. There was a large stone fireplace resembling that of the others in town, but the décor was rustic Mexican cantina rather than mountain lodge. There was a long wooden bar with brightly colored ceramic bowls filled with chips and salsa. The tables were made of rough wood and were surrounded by benches rather than chairs. There were brightly colored tapestries hanging from the walls and brightly colored lights hung from the ceiling. Mariachi music played softly in the background.

They discarded their hats, gloves, and jackets in the mudroom before walking toward a table for six near the fireplace.

"This place is great." Alyson stood in front of the roaring fire, trying to thaw out. Her hands and feet were numb and she was fairly certain her face had frozen into a permanent smile.

Mac grabbed a menu and stood next to Alyson with her back to the dancing flames. "And the food looks like it's to die for. I'm leaning toward the beef burrito."

"I've tried those. They're excellent," Devon assured her.

A pretty dark-haired waitress brought glasses of water and baskets of warm tortilla chips and freshly made salsa. Due to the late hour the restaurant was pretty much deserted. Most of the resort guests had retreated either to the pub, which was filled to capacity, or to their rooms to wait out the storm.

"I'm not sure I can remember ever being so cold." Alyson held her hands in front of the fire.

Devon vigorously rubbed Alyson's arms in an effort to help stimulate circulation.

"You should wear thermal underwear under your clothes. The layers help hold in body heat."

"Now you tell me. So did you find out what happened to the dead guy in the snowbank?" Alyson sat down on the bench closest to the fire as the feeling started to return to her limbs. She dipped a tortilla chip in the spicy salsa and tried not to shiver as she chewed.

"I'm not sure. A couple walking back to their cabin from the village saw a foot sticking up out of the snow. The body was otherwise completely covered. The security guard I spoke to said the man appeared to have frozen to death."

"I thought the guy had his throat slit." Mac broke one of the salty chips in half. "Or possibly he was shot or strangled; I'm not sure. The chatter I've heard seems to be inconclusive to this point."

"That's what the rumor mill suggested," Trevor joined in, "but according to the security patrol the death appears to have been accidental."

"The security guy seemed to think the man had a little bit too much to drink, passed out, fell, and was covered by the snow," Eli added. "He said that happens more often than you might think."

"Really? People just get drunk and freeze to death?" Mac scooted closer to Eli, in an attempt to share body warmth, Alyson assumed.

"The temperatures up here can dip into dangerous territory pretty quickly," Devon pointed out. "The air temperature dropped forty degrees when the blizzard blew in a couple of hours ago. Most people weren't prepared for it. There's a ton of literature in all the rooms warning about the danger of hypothermia, but most people don't bother to read it."

"Forty degrees. Wow, that's a lot." Alyson took a sip of her water. "Any word on how long this storm is supposed to last?"

"At least a couple of days," Devon answered. "Sorry. I know you were looking forward to skiing, but the house we're staying in is nice. Huge fireplace, outdoor hot tub, fantastic views."

"Sounds cozy."

"Yeah, cozy," Trevor complained. "The ultimate love nest for the five of us. Maybe I should have invited Chelsea."

"No!" Alyson and Mac shouted simultaneously.

"It's going to be awkward being a fifth wheel the whole trip."

"We need to get you a girl," Mac mused. "I'm sure there are a lot of single hotties at the resort who would be glad to round out our little group."

"Speaking of hotties, who's that who just walked in?" Trevor asked.

A petite blonde with waist-length hair and a tight-cropped sweater walked in with three other teenage girls. They were laughing about something one of them had said as they hung up their parkas.

"Which one?" Eli asked.

"The blonde."

"Her name's Andi," Eli supplied. "She's the resort owner's daughter."

"Does she have a boyfriend?" Trevor wondered.

"Not that I know of."

"All of a sudden this trip got more interesting."

Alyson saw Trevor watching the girl as she reached up to adjust her turtleneck, exposing a strip of skin between her sweater and her jeans. She had to admit she had a nice figure. Coupled with her long hair and nice smile, she was exactly the type Trevor would go for.

"Wipe the drool off your face, she coming over," Mac warned Trevor.

Andi's friends headed toward a table in the corner while Andi came toward their table near the fireplace.

"Hi, guys. Who are your friends?" Andi asked Devon and Eli.

"This is my girlfriend, Alyson, and Eli's girlfriend, Mackenzie," Devon introduced them. "The handsome guy drooling at the end of the table is our friend Trevor."

"Glad to meet you." Andi was looking directly at Trevor.

"The pleasure is all mine." Trevor grabbed her hand and kissed the back of it.

Alyson rolled her eyes.

"We were just about to order some dinner. Would you care to join us?" Trevor asked.

"Well..." Andi hesitated. "I'm here with my friends. But hey, why not? I'll just go tell them what I'm doing. I'll be right back."

Andi started toward the table where her friends were waiting. After explaining things to her friends, she sat down on the bench next to Trevor.

"We were just talking about the man they found in the snowbank," Trevor said. "Rumor we heard was that he froze to death."

"Yeah, that's what we think. People don't realize how dangerous the elements can be. We have quite a few deaths every year at the resort and it's always a nightmare. Families come here to have fun and relax, and then someone ends up dead."

"People freeze to death often?" Mac asked.

"Not really. Most accidents happen on the slopes. Skiing is a dangerous sport, and unfortunately, there are more skier-meets-tree accidents than anyone realizes. We also have our share of backwoods avalanches that out-of-bounds skiers and snowmobile riders sometimes get caught in. A heavy snow like we're having right now is a key trigger. You guys should be careful and stay on the groomed runs."

"Are the local police going to investigate the death even though it appears to be accidental?" Alyson asked. "I mean, there's always the possibility that the guy didn't pass out but was knocked out."

"We don't really have a police force per se, just a security patrol. Usually someone from Vancouver comes in to investigate crimes, but no one will be able to fly in until the storm passes. From what I hear, that could be days."

"Can't they drive in the way we came?" Alyson asked.

"Didn't you hear? There's been a snowslide; a pretty big one, from what I heard. The road will be closed until they can get it cleared. I'm afraid we're on our own for the next few days."

"You mean we're trapped here?" Mac asked. "No one can get in and no one can get out?"

"Don't worry. We're completely self-contained. We have our own shopping, restaurants, entertainment, fueling stations, and medical facility. We even have our own volunteer fire department. Barring a real emergency, we should be fine."

"How do you power all this?" Alyson asked. "I don't remember seeing electrical lines when we came in."

"The terrain is too rugged to run electricity. We have several alternate energy sources: propane-powered generators, solar power, even wind power. We're really cutting edge."

"What about phone service?" Mac asked. "I noticed my cell doesn't work here."

"We have a satellite system that works pretty well except when there's a big storm like this one. If the satphones are out we rely on two-way radios. It's not always the most convenient system, but most guests come here to get away from it all, so lack of phone service usually isn't a problem. We do have the occasional workaholic who goes into withdrawal during storms. Usually when the phones are down we can't get Internet service either."

"Does that happen often?" Mac asked. "Total isolation from the rest of the world?"

"No, not really. I mean, we have storms and lose the phones several times a year, but I can't ever remember having a slide that completely blocked the road the way this one has. I'm afraid the staff really has their hands full with this one. We have guests who are due to check out who can't leave and others who have prepaid for rooms they can't get to."

Alyson looked up as the waitress returned to the table. She was dressed in a brightly colored dress that fit in perfectly with the décor.

"Can I take your order?" she asked.

"I'll have the fish tacos," Alyson ordered.

"Beef burrito for me," Trevor said.

"Same here," Eli agreed.

"I was going to have the burrito, but now I'm thinking chicken tacos," Mac informed the woman.

"I'll have the chicken tacos as well," Devon ordered.

"Andi?" the girl asked.

"A taco salad."

"Have you heard anything more about Mario's condition?" the waitress asked Andi.

"No, nothing yet. I'll let you know if I do. How's Carmen taking it?"

"Pretty hard, as you can imagine. As soon as I finish my shift I'm going to go over and check on her."

"Mario?" Alyson asked after the waitress walked away.

"One of the propane tanks exploded yesterday," Andi explained. "No one knows exactly what happened, but apparently there was a small explosion that threw a maintenance worker, Mario Gonzales, into a snowbank and caused third-degree burns over much of his body. He was airlifted to the hospital in Vancouver. No one's heard whether he's going to make it or not. He was hurt really bad."

"Had the tank been tampered with?" Alyson asked.

"No one's sure yet. All of the propane tanks on the property are inspected and tested on a regular basis. There's no reason the accident would have occurred if tampering hadn't been present, but at this point there's no way to know."

"What do people think happened?" Alyson asked.

"Some of the guys from the maintenance crew were here earlier. They swear the tank in question was inspected last week. The consensus is that someone tampered with the tank, but for the life of me I can't imagine why anyone would want to hurt Mario. He's the nicest guy in the world. The whole thing was probably some freak accident. I just hope Mario's okay."

"Do you think the body in the snowbank is somehow related?" Mac asked. "I mean, two freak accidents in two days?"

"I hadn't thought of that," Andi answered. "You aren't suggesting that someone is doing all of this on purpose, are you?"

"With our luck, I think there most definitely may be more to the story than two random accidents," Mac said.

"Unfortunately, this sounds like an *us* situation. Come for a pleasant ski holiday and end up trapped with a serial killer at a remote mountain resort in the middle of a blizzard."

"This kind of thing happens to you all often?" Andi asked.

"You'd be surprised." Mac groaned.

"Come on, don't scare Andi," Trevor cautioned her. "Our little group does seem to have a propensity for finding trouble if trouble is to be found, but I'm sure the two accidents were just a freaky coincidence."

"I hope so," Andi stated. "Until the road opens or the storm clears, we're totally trapped. If there is someone out there causing these accidents we could be in real trouble. I should talk to my dad."

"Just to be on the safe side, maybe we should do a little investigation," Alyson suggested. "Without the presence of a real police force, I'd say we're as experienced as anyone."

"You guys detectives or something?" Andi wondered.

"Something." Alyson leaned in and lowered her voice. "It's not like we went to school and chose solving mysteries as a profession, but somehow we keep finding ourselves immersed in events beyond our control. Just last week we found a missing person, solved a murder, and uncovered a conspiracy."

"You're kidding."

"I wish I was. It's been our experience that seemingly random acts usually end up following a pattern."

"Okay, then. I'll help you any way I can. I have access to pretty much everything on the resort. It's probably better to keep this to ourselves, though. If my dad found out that his one and only offspring was doing something that could potentially put her in danger he'd put a stop to it right away."

The conversation was interrupted as the waitress brought steaming plates of spicy burritos, tacos, refried beans, and Spanish rice. "Can I get you anything else?"

"No, I think we're fine. Everything looks excellent, as always," Andi answered. "If you do get over to talk to Carmen tell her my prayers are with her brother."

"I'll do that," the waitress answered. "It's hard with the storm. We haven't been able to get through to the hospital, so we don't really know what's going on."

"I think my dad has been in touch with Vancouver on the two-way radio. You should check with him."

"Thanks, I will."

"So where do we start?" Andi asked after the waitress had walked away.

"I'd like to get a look at the body." Alyson picked up one of her tacos. "After we eat of course."

Chapter 2

"I'm pretty sure they took the body to the clinic," Andi informed them as they ate their meal. "It'll be closed now, but I have a passkey that opens any lock on the resort."

"Oh, good, no breaking and entering this time around," Mac breathed.

"Breaking and entering?" Andi asked.

"Last week, during our investigation into the mayor's death and his secretary's disappearance, we had to break into several of the town offices," Trevor explained. "Mac wasn't totally comfortable with the whole thing, but we got our guy."

"I guess you did what you needed to do. But that shouldn't be a problem this time. That doesn't mean we won't need to be sneaky, though. I'm not sure how I'd explain to my dad our need to pay a visit to the clinic at this late hour."

"We'll be extrastealthy," Alyson promised. "Have there been any other accidents in the past few weeks?"

"No, things have been pretty quiet. In fact, the last real accident we had at the resort happened last spring. A skier died in an avalanche and, unlike most avalanche mishaps, this one was in bounds. We're in the middle of a lawsuit over the whole thing as we speak. The victim's family is asserting that the resort was negligent because it didn't take all necessary precautions to prevent the avalanche."

"Precautions?" Mac asked.

"We have an avalanche patrol team that's one of the best anywhere. There are certain conditions that increase the likelihood of an avalanche: warm weather, heavy snow, rain followed by snow. If an avalanche danger exists, precautions are taken. Usually we use explosives to create a controlled avalanche, thereby decreasing the likelihood of a natural occurrence. Sometimes sections of the resort, usually those with the steepest terrain, will be closed until the threat diminishes. This is a ski resort; accidents happen, but our safety record is one of the best around."

"So why did the family think the resort was negligent?" Alyson asked.

"My dad says that sometimes people in deep grief need to have someone to blame for their suffering."

"Do you think they have a case?" Mac wondered.

"Not really. We've already been through an arbitration process, which ruled in our favor. The family is insisting on a jury trial, so we aren't totally off the hook. In fact, there's a team of safety experts here this week to conduct an audit of our safety practices and procedures. Devon and Eli's dad installed software that helped my dad get ready for it. I'm hoping everything will come out okay. If we lose this lawsuit, we could lose the resort. I'm not sure our insurance would cover us if negligence is proven."

"So this isn't a good time for unexplained accidents," Alyson concluded.

"Tell me about it. You never know which way a jury will go, and any little piece of evidence, no matter if it's real or fabricated, could be the deciding factor in a trial."

"You don't think someone from the family who's suing you is creating these accidents, do you?" Trevor asked. "To provide them with ammunition?"

"God, I hope not. One man is dead and Mario might not make it. If someone is doing this on purpose, we have a real sicko on our hands."

"I guess all we can do is find out what actually happened to both Mario and the man in the snowbank, and, if there has been foul play, who did it and why," Alyson said. "If someone is orchestrating these accidents there's bound to be a link. All we need to do is find it."

Devon picked up the check. "I'll pay this and then we'll head over to the clinic. If someone is causing these accidents we need to figure it out as soon as we can."

By the time they arrived at the clinic it was completely dark and deserted. Andi unlocked the back door and they slipped in.

"Better not turn on the lights until we get to the interior rooms," Andi suggested. "I know my way around, so just follow me and walk carefully."

Andi grabbed Trevor's hand, who in turn grabbed Mac's, who grabbed Eli's, and so forth, with Devon bringing up the rear. They walked slowly down a hall and around a corner before coming to a locked room. Andi unlocked the door and went inside. Once everyone was in, she closed the door and turned on the light.

"Don't worry; there are no outside windows in here, so no one will see us. We just need to be careful not to disturb anything. Dr. Mark is a stickler for order."

A body, covered by a white sheet, was laid out on the examination table. The room was a typical doctor's office, with shelves full of gauze and bandages and locked drawers full of syringes and vials of common drugs. A blood pressure monitor hung from one wall, and a portable overhead light stood off to the side.

Alyson pulled a box of white rubber gloves off one of the shelves and passed them around. "Everyone put on a pair of these. We don't want to leave fingerprints all over Dr. Mark's sterile room."

Alyson walked over to the body and pulled the sheet away from the victim's head and shoulders. He was totally colorless except for the tinge of blue around his eyes and lips. He had dark hair and was clean-shaven and appeared to be in his mid to late thirties. Alyson closed her eyes and fought a wave of nausea as she carefully tilted his head to the side in order to get a better look at the back of his head and neck.

She ran her fingers over his skull in an attempt to determine whether there were any cuts or contusions. "I feel a bump. Here on the left side."

Devon ran his fingers over the same spot. "There's no blood. He could have just hit his head when he fell."

"Let me take a look." Mac walked around to the opposite side of the table. "The only way a fall could cause a bump like that is if his head hit a rock or something hard."

"I guess we could go back to the scene to check it out, although with the way it's snowing, any evidence is sure to have already been covered up."

Mac pulled the sheet down to the man's waist and searched his torso for additional evidence of foul play. His chest and arms appeared to be free of cuts or bruising. She picked up his hand and looked under his fingernails. "Someone see if they can find a pair of tweezers and a Petri dish, or maybe a vial of some type."

Andi started looking through the drawers on one end of the room while Trevor searched the other. The group were totally quiet as they went about their business as professionally as possible.

"Got 'em." Andi handed Mac a pair of tweezers and a small vial that would typically be used to take a blood sample.

Mac carefully removed a small particle from beneath the victim's nail. "Looks like skin. I don't suppose this facility has a lab?"

"The medical lab is down the hall," Andi answered.

"Okay, one of you guys might want to take a look beneath the sheet to see if there are any other cuts or bruises. I'll take this sample to the lab to see if I can figure out exactly what it is."

"I'm coming with you," Alyson volunteered. "I'm not sure I want to be here to witness the more delicate part of the examination."

Alyson, Mac, and Andi walked carefully down the hall toward the fully equipped medical lab. As before, they left the lights in the hallway off and followed Andi through the darkened corridor.

"Wow, I'm impressed," Mac commented as they snuck in and turned on the light. The room was fully equipped, with an X-ray machine, microscopes, an ultrasound machine, and a variety of other expensive-looking equipment.

"I told you, we need to be pretty self-contained. Minor accidents such as broken bones and cuts and abrasions can be treated right here. Dr. Mark has even been known to deliver a baby now and then, and perform minor surgery when needed. The really serious cases are airlifted to Vancouver."

"Like Mario," Mac said.

"I'm afraid third-degree burns are a little beyond Dr. Mark's ability to treat here. It's a good thing the accident happened yesterday, when we were able to get air service. If the explosion had happened after the storm rolled in I'm not sure what we would have done. There's no way the Evac chopper would have been able to fly in this storm."

"From what you've said I take it Mario's injuries were pretty extensive." Mac began to look around for the supplies she'd need.

"He's got burns over a large part of his body. My dad says that even if he does survive, his rehabilitation will be quite extensive. Aunt Veronica is arranging for housing near the hospital for his family. It's doubtful Mario will ever be able to return to work. The resort is making sure his family is taken care of."

"It's nice the resort is going to so much trouble to make his family comfortable," Alyson commented. "A lot of employers wouldn't take on so much responsibility."

"Mario's family. All of our employees are. When you live in isolated conditions you get close to people pretty fast."

Mac continued looking through the drawers for something she could use to identify the particle she had removed from the victim. "Exactly how many people are on the grounds at any one time?"

"On weeks like this, when we're filled to capacity, around twelve hundred. Possibly more. We have two lodges, the Grizzly Mountain Lodge, which you saw in town, and the Moose Lake Lodge, which is a ski-in, ski-out lodge near the lifts. The Grizzly

Mountain Lodge has two hundred and fifty rooms and Moose Lake Lodge has one hundred twenty. In addition to that, we have the cabins that are tucked into the surrounding forest, as well as the bigger lodgings, such as the one where you're staying. Depending on how many people are in each room, the lodges alone can hold around seven hundred people. The cabins often house groups of four to six, and the houses can hold up to ten or twelve. Then of course there are the two hundred or so employees who live on-site."

"Wow, that's a lot." Mac pulled a chair up to one of the microscopes. "Are all of your employees single? I mean, it must be hard to raise a family in such an isolated place."

"No, we have families living here. It's isolated, but to be honest that's what attracts a lot of our families. They want their kids to grow up without all the negative distractions that are found in the cities."

"What about school?" Alyson asked.

"We have our own school. Well, at least until seventh grade. After that some kids are homeschooled, and some go to boarding school in Calgary or Vancouver, which is what I do. Some families relocate at that point."

"Is it hard to leave your family and go away to school?" Mac wondered. "As big of a pain in the butt as my family sometimes is, I think I'd miss them if I didn't see them for weeks at a time."

"It's okay. It was hard at first, but I have good friends at school, and I'm home all summer and on school holidays. I do miss my dad sometimes, and my Aunt Ronnie."

"And your mom?" Mac asked.

"She left when I was four. I see her occasionally. She lives in France with her fourth husband. He's only eight years older than I am."

"Eight years? Really? Is that weird? I mean for you. How'd they meet?" Alyson asked.

Andi shrugged. "He's twenty-four, she's thirty-six. He's a photographer and my mom is a model. They met on a shoot. From what I hear, it was love at first sight. He's a nice enough guy, certainly better than husband number three, who was a sixty-four-year-old lawyer with the disposition of a feral cat. But sometimes the age thing is strange. I mean, I'm closer to this guy's age than my mom is.

And he's a total babe. It's hard to think of him as 'Daddy.'"

"I see your point." Mac used an eyedropper to apply a solution to the sample. "The whole situation must be really hard on you."

She shrugged again. "It's okay. I have my dad and he's great. Seriously, the best dad ever. And I have my Aunt Veronica, Ronnie for short. She's my dad's younger sister. She's been dating Dr. Mark for about ten years. I keep hoping they'll get married and provide me with a couple of cousins, but so far no go."

"Wow, ten years is a long time to date and not take it to the next level." Alyson stood behind Mac, watching what she was doing over her shoulder.

"Tell me about it. I'm not sure what the problem is. They're both really great people and they seem to really love each other. I asked Aunt Ronnie about it once and she just said it was complicated. Whatever that means."

"I think I've got it," Mac interrupted. "It's definitely skin. I guess we should hang on to this in case the police decide to do an investigation."

"Any way to tell whose skin?" Andi asked.

"Not without DNA testing and a possible match," Mac told her.

"So what are we thinking?" Alyson asked. "That our victim was in a struggle before his death and scratched someone?"

"Possibly. Of course he could also have been in a bar fight or even scratched himself at some point. Short of additional evidence, I'd say we're at a standstill. Let's get back to the guys to see if they found any other evidence.

Devon, Trevor, and Eli were sitting on the counters discussing the latest basketball stats when the girls returned. They seemed to be in a fairly heated discussion as to which team was due to reach the finals that year. Devon seemed to favor the Lakers, although it sounded like his opinion was in the minority.

"Did you find anything?" Mac interrupted.

"No. We couldn't find any evidence of foul play," Trevor said. "Maybe the guy really did freeze to death. It's certainly cold enough to cause hypothermia in a pretty short amount of time, especially if the victim was unconscious."

"Maybe. At this point I'd say the evidence is pretty inconclusive. Maybe we should ask around at the bar tomorrow, see if anyone remembers anything," Mac suggested. "Do we have a name or any other personal information about the victim?"

"Not that I know of. I'll ask around," Andi volunteered. "I could check with registration; they should have basic check-in data. Maybe we could meet up in the morning. The coffee shop has excellent pancakes. Say around nine?"

"Sounds good," Trevor answered for the group. "How about we give you a ride home?"

"That would be awesome. It's not far; just up the road, actually. I usually walk pretty much everywhere I go, but with the storm, I'm not all that anxious to make the trek."

Devon dropped Andi off at her house and headed back through town. All of the buildings were constructed of real wooden logs and each had a coil of smoke spiraling out of chimneys constructed from various shades of river rock. The town had been decorated for the holiday with white lights, evergreen boughs, and large red bows.

The giant Christmas tree that stood in the center of the town square swayed to and fro as many of the colored lights, red and green balls, and decorated pine cones blew across the snow-covered roadway. Snow was piled high against a huge stone and the wood sign that announced you were entering Grizzly Mountain Resort.

"I bet the town was a Christmas fairy land before the storm hit," Alyson commented. "Based on the decorations that are scattered all over the ground, it looks like they went all out."

"Yeah, it was really pretty." Devon squeezed Alyson's hand between them. "I'm sorry you missed it."

"Is the resort open year-round? Andi mentioned that entire families live here."

"Yeah. In the winter there's skiing, both downhill and cross-country, ice-skating, snowmobile rides, snowshoeing, and other snow sports. In the summer they have hiking, fishing, rock climbing, mountain biking, canoeing, and other warm-weather sports. There's even a golf course buried underneath the nordic ski track."

"I bet it would be beautiful in the summer," Alyson imagined.

"Right now I'd be happy to get a peek at the winter landscape. With this storm I've barely been able to see a few feet in front of me," Mac complained from her second-row seat.

"Don't worry. I'm sure it will clear up in a day or two." Eli put his arm around her and pulled her close. "In the meantime I can think of a few other things we can do to stay occupied."

"Oh, yeah? Like what?"

Eli whispered in her ear and Mac giggled.

"Hey, you guys, knock it off," Trevor complained. "No talk of smoochies unless Andi or some other equally hot chick is around for me."

"Who said we were talking about smoochies?" Mac defended herself. "For your information we were talking about playing board games."

"Yeah, right."

"We're here." Devon pulled up in front of a two-story house, constructed with the familiar log and rock exteriors of the rest of the buildings on the resort. The roofline was strung with white lights and there was a large Christmas tree showing through the picture windows that lined the front of the house.

Huge drifts of snow had piled up in front of the structure and the walkway was almost completely concealed beneath the blowing snow.

"Watch your step walking into the house. I shoveled the walkway earlier, but you'd never know that now. It's bound to be slippery," Devon warned. "Mac and Alyson can share a room." Devon grabbed

Alyson's bags and walked ahead of the rest of them through the large entry and up the stairs. "Trevor can share with Eli and I'll bunk in with my dad. Each room has two double beds and its own bath."

"Wow, this place is gorgeous." Mac looked around at the cathedral ceilings, rustic furniture, and warm evergreen color scheme as she followed Eli, who was carrying her bags up the wide staircase.

The floors were all polished wood with thick green and brown rugs. Every exterior wall was framed with large picture windows and green and brown drapes. There was a huge stone fireplace in the living area that towered two floors high and boasted a real log mantel that was decorated with candles, greenery, and antiques.

The bedroom to which Devon showed Ali and Mac had two double beds covered with heavy down comforters, a large pine armoire, twin night tables with pine lamps, and two overstuffed chairs beside a small rock fireplace. The floor was carpeted with plush forest carpeting and the walls were paneled with natural pine.

"The bathroom is right through this door," Devon indicated. "Go ahead and get changed and unpacked, then meet us downstairs in the living room. I'll start a fire. I think we could all use a hot drink to thaw out."

Mac kissed Eli as he set down her bags. "Thanks. I'm glad we're finally here. I've missed you. I hope we'll get to spend some time together, just the two of us."

"Me too." Eli kissed her back. Tucking a strand of her long red hair behind her ear, he smiled at her and kissed her again. "Me too."

"Check out this tub," Alyson called as Mac closed the door behind Eli's departing form. "It's even got Jacuzzi jets."

"Perfect for all your little sore parts at the end of the day. Eli mentioned that there's an outdoor hot tub on the back deck. Sounds very romantic. Of course it never occurred to me to bring a bathing suit on a ski trip, but he says there's a shop in town that sells them. I thought we could check it out tomorrow."

"Let's unpack and get downstairs. The thought of curling up by the fire with something hot to drink, watching the snow, and having pleasant conversation with the people I love most sounds like heaven on earth."

"Pleasant conversation?" Mac snorted. "You know the guys are going to want to strategize. Give them a good mystery to solve and they become single-minded."

"For tonight, we'll put a ban on shop talk. We've done what we could tonight. Tomorrow's soon enough to jump into research mode. For tonight I'm thinking soft music, a warm fire, and pleasant conversation."

"Sounds good to me."

After they unpacked, Mac and Alyson joined the guys by the fire in the great room. When Alyson had pictured this setting during the previous week, snow had been falling gently outside and the biggest concern she had was which ski run to start off with the following day. The reality was a storm that continued to blow angrily, completely obstructing the view outside the large floor-to-ceiling windows and a boyfriend who had already started making notes for the next day's investigation. She took the notepad away from Devon and pulled him toward the large rock fireplace, where a fire danced merrily in tune to the soft jazz someone had put on the expensive stereo system.

She wrapped her arms around his neck and kissed him as she swayed to the music. "Mac and I have declared a moratorium on death and frozen corpses for tonight," she whispered against his lips.

"Sounds good," Devon groaned.

"I'm going to show Mac the rest of the house." Eli grabbed her hand and started walking toward the hallway leading to the kitchen and dining area.

"There's a rest of the house?" Trevor asked as they disappeared down the hall.

"Not really. Just the kitchen."

"I think he wanted for them to be alone," Alyson guessed.

"Yeah, Eli's been all nervous about the gift he got for her: a birthstone necklace. Sapphire."

"But Mac's birthday is in January. January is garnet," Alyson pointed out

"Sapphire is for September. He said that because he met her in September, he considers that the birth of their relationship."

"Oh, that's so sweet." Alyson handed Devon the gift she had brought for him. "Tasteful, but not nearly as touching as Eli's gift. I hope you like it."

Devon took the box and handed one to Alyson in return. They both opened them at the same time to reveal cashmere sweaters. "Oh, it's perfect," they said in unison.

"Feeling a little left out over here," Trevor teased.

"Eli and I got a little something for you." Devon handed Trevor a brightly wrapped box.

"Really, for me? You shouldn't have. Really." He tore open the package. "Oh, wow. Thanks. They're great." Trevor slipped on the pair of dark sunglasses.

"Actually, they were Mac's idea. Eli called her to ask what to get. She said you needed a pair."

"I so did. Thanks a lot."

Alyson and Devon curled up on the love seat.

"Uh, maybe I should head up to bed." Trevor started to stand up.

"No, stay," Alyson said persuasively. "We'll make some hot drinks and catch up on the past couple of weeks. I just want to take a minute to relax in this beautiful house with my friends. All of my friends. I've missed having us all together."

"Okay, if you're sure. I'll get the drinks," Trevor offered.

"I'm not actually sure how we're going to have a conversation without using the words *death* or *corpse*." Devon kissed Alyson's neck.

"Yeah, I guess that was a stretch."

"I'd really like to hear about your adventure last week. When the others get back. For now, I'd just like to kiss you."

"Sounds like a plan."

Chapter 3

The next morning they went to the café for breakfast. It was decorated as charmingly as the rest of the resort, with red-and-white-checkered tablecloths covering round tables surrounded by old-fashioned chrome and red vinyl chairs. The matching curtains were pulled back, offering a view of blowing snow and near whiteout conditions. On one side of the room, an old-fashioned counter was lined with red vinyl-covered stools, facing the kitchen through an open cook's window. On the other side of the café, a vintage ice cream counter encircled an old-fashioned soda fountain. Fifties music played in the background as waitresses in poodle skirts waited on tables.

"Have you heard anything more about Mario?" Alyson asked Andi as she drizzled syrup on fluffy buttermilk pancakes.

"He's still in intensive care, but they've managed to stabilize him. I hope he's going to be okay. It's hard getting updates. The phone lines are down, but the two-way radios are working okay. My dad's been talking to a good friend of his in Vancouver who's been checking in on him. Hopefully the storm will lighten up a little and we can get through directly."

"I hope he's going to be okay," Trevor sympathized.

"Me too." Andi smiled at him.

"It's really snowing out there," Mac added. "How much do you think we've gotten since last night?"

"Several feet. My dad said the national weather service is predicting upward of ten feet by the time this is all over. I'm afraid your first day at our resort won't be quite the ski holiday you imagined."

"Yeah, it doesn't look like it," Mac agreed.

"The resort has several indoor activities scheduled," Andi offered. "It helps to keep the guests from getting too restless. There's bingo in the lobby of the main lodge and a complimentary movie in the theater. I think they've got something going in the pizza parlor too. Not exactly a day on the slopes, but if you're bored..."

"Thanks, but I thought we'd head over to the bar and start asking around about the dead guy," Alyson informed her. "As long as we can't ski we may as well investigate. It'd be nice to get this wrapped up by the time the slopes open."

"The bar doesn't open until two. We can go then. In the meantime, we can see if Hank, the bartender, is available to talk to us. I found out the dead guy's name was Bruce Long. He'd been a guest for several days. He was here alone; no friends or family. His registration paperwork shows that he lived in Calgary and visited here once before, around this time last year. I wrote down the address and phone number he used to check in. Oh, and he used a credit card to secure the room. I got the number. If the Internet ever comes back up we should be able to use it to check on prior activity. At least I guess we can. Veronica Mars always seemed to be able to get information like that."

"Wow, I'm impressed," Alyson complimented. "I can see you're going to fit right in with our group. It's not everyone who could have found out so much in such a short amount of time."

"Well, it helps to know people. Oh, and I also found out he was staying in one of the cabins up the road. Maybe we could check it out. I'm pretty sure no one's been in to clean it up yet."

"Sounds like we have a good start." Alyson poured herself a second cup of coffee. "We should visit the cabin first, just in case someone from housekeeping does decide to do some cleaning. Then we'll look up the bartender. Later, we can stop by the bar to talk to the other patrons."

"If the Internet does come back up I should be able to handle that credit card lead," Mac said. "We can also Google him to see if anything pops up."

"All we need is for the storm to clear enough for the satellite signal to get through," Andi informed her. "Even with big storms, there are often small breaks in the weather. We'll need to be ready to jump on it if one occurs."

"What about Mario's accident?" Trevor mixed his hash browns with his cut-up egg. "If we suspect foul play, shouldn't we be investigating that too?"

"I'm not sure what we can do," Alyson responded. "I guess we could check out the scene."

"It's under four feet of fresh snow," Eli reminded her. "If there was any evidence of foul play I doubt we'd be able to find it now."

"We could check out the maintenance shop," Andi suggested. "Maybe Mario left something behind. Notes or something."

"Did anyone witness the accident?" Mac asked. "Another employee, maybe a guest?"

"I'm not sure. We can ask around," Andi said. "Someone must have seen something. It was Christmas Day, though, and most of the guests must have been occupied with family and friends. I don't think there were a lot of people out and about."

"Okay, here's an obvious detective question," Devon joined in. "As far as you know, Andi, could there be a connection between Mario and Bruce Long? Are they friends? Did they ever work together? You said Bruce was here last year. Could they have met then?"

"I guess. I really don't know. It's a good angle to check out, though. Maybe Carmen would know. Or maybe Charlie, one of the other maintenance workers; he and Mario are pretty good friends."

"So how's your dad holding up through all this?" Trevor asked. "With the safety audit going on, he must be pretty stressed out."

"He's not loving it, but he's okay. So far none of the investigators have found any safety violations. The fact that two accidents have occurred in the past few days is odd but not setting off any alarms, apparently. Honestly, at this point I think we're the only ones to suspect foul play."

"Other than the family that's suing you, can you think of anyone who might want to cause trouble for the resort?" Alyson asked.

"I have an uncle who's engaged in a feud with my family, but I doubt he'd murder anyone. Besides, he's not here."

"A feud over what?" Trevor asked.

"The resort was originally built by my great-grandfather. On his death, my grandfather and his siblings, my Great-Uncle Bobby and my Great-Aunt Alexis, each inherited a third. Bobby had a bit of a gambling problem and needed cash, so he sold his share to my grandfather. When my grandfather passed away last year he left his two thirds of the resort to my father and my Aunt Ronnie. Apparently, Great-Uncle Bobby thought his share should have come back to him. I could almost see him doing something to cause trouble for the resort, but murder? That's pretty serious."

"Does your great-uncle have money now?" Mac asked.

"Not that I know of. Why?"

"Because, if he did have access to some cash, he might be able to get the resort back if the pending lawsuit causes a financial hardship. My guess is that the family suing the resort wants cold hard cash, not stock in the resort."

"So Great-Uncle Bobby could probably buy it from them at a huge discount?"

"Exactly."

"I don't know. It's a good theory, but I don't know how he'd get the money."

"Unless he has a partner," Eli speculated.

"I guess. He always was a bit of a player. My dad said he used to scam people out of money all the time to cover his gambling debts."

"I don't think we should take him off the suspect list," Eli said. "Right now I think we need to keep an open mind."

"Well, if we're making a list of all possible suspects we should add Truman Montgomery. He's one of our closest competitors. He's been trying to buy the resort for years. My grandfather refused to sell it to him and since he died and my dad is running the place he's been working on him big-time."

"Has your dad shown any interest in selling?" Alyson asked.

"No, but that won't keep Truman from trying. I'm sure if there were a financial hardship, Truman would swoop in and try to buy the place out from under us. Great-Aunt Alexis still owns a third of the resort and she's already made some noise about wanting to sell. I'm sure she wouldn't do anything against my dad and Aunt Ronnie's wishes, but if the situation presented itself, I think she could be convinced. She lives in New York and doesn't have the same love of the place the rest of us do. To her, the resort is just an investment."

"She must have grown up here," Alyson pointed out.

"She did, but the minute she was old enough to leave she did. She rarely visits, and when she does it's usually because of some business meeting she can't get out of."

"So Truman gets added to the suspect list," Eli concluded.

"You know," Trevor realized, "if Bruce Long was murdered the killer is probably still here. The slide happened shortly before the body was found. I doubt he or she would have had time to get out."

"Oh, that's a comforting thought." Mac lay her head on Eli's shoulder. "I guess we'd better keep our eyes open. If there is a killer and that person is still on the grounds he probably won't appreciate us snooping around."

"We just need to be careful so that no one knows what we're doing," Alyson said.

"If we assume the two men were the victims of a killer or killers and the motive was to sabotage the resort, who else should we add to the list?" Devon asked.

Andi leaned back in the booth. Her brow was furrowed, as if she was considering the question.

"There is one person who comes to mind, but it's a long shot. While most of our employees love us there was an incident a while back. One of the women who works in the administration office was accused of siphoning funds from the cash drawers that are distributed each day. Based on the testimony of several other employees, as well as the timing of the missing cash, it seemed obvious she must be the guilty party, but my dad was never able to catch her red-handed. He didn't want to fire her without conclusive proof, but he also didn't want her to have continued access to the cash, so he transferred her to another position. The woman claimed she was being harassed and threatened a lawsuit if my dad didn't return her to her former job."

"Did he?" Alyson asked.

"No. The cash drawers had been turning up short for months, but the minute the woman was transferred they started balancing. The woman ended up quitting her job and moving away, but not before she made sure everyone knew she planned to get even for the injustice she felt she'd suffered."

"Sounds like motive to me," Mac commented.

"Yes, but as far as I know she's not here at the resort. However..."

"However?" Alyson asked.

"She does have several close friends who still work here. If she happened to be staying with one of them I suppose it's possible she could be on-site and we wouldn't know about it."

"Maybe you should ask around," Trevor suggested.

"Yeah, I'll do that."

"In the meantime, I suggest we find out what we can about the victims and look for a motive other than resort sabotage," Devon suggested.

"I agree with Dev." Alyson nodded. "It's much too early in the investigation to focus in on any one motive or suspect. Chances are the incidences are unrelated, but if they aren't, we need to find a link."

Chapter 4

The cabin where Bruce Long had been staying was just down the road from the pub. The body had been found about halfway between the two, supporting the theory that the man was simply walking home, passed out, and froze to death. After breakfast the gang walked the short distance to the cabin through the still raging storm.

"Maybe we should have driven." Alyson wiped the snow off her shoulder and shook out her knit cap after Andi unlocked the door and ushered them all inside.

"The SUV's still at the restaurant. I can go back to get it," Devon offered.

"That's okay; with all this snow there's nowhere to park." Alyson stomped the snow off her feet, creating a small pile of snow on the hardwood floor of the small but cozy cabin.

"We have a crew that plows out the drives of the guest cabins, but I guess they didn't bother with this one because its occupant won't be needing his car," Andi said.

"Okay, everyone look around for anything that might be a clue, but be careful not to disturb anything you don't have to," Mac instructed.

"What exactly are we looking for?" Trevor asked.

"I don't know. Anything that might give us a clue as to who the victim was, what he was doing here, or who might have killed him."

The closet and dresser drawers were full of clothes, both casual and dressy. The bathroom counter was littered with the usual personal grooming supplies and the drawer of the bedside table held round-trip tickets from Calgary. Beneath the ticket stubs was a file folder with receipts from charges made during his stay at the resort, as well as a car rental contract dated four days earlier. According to the contract, he had planned to return the car on the twenty-eighth.

"If Mr. Long lived in Calgary I wonder why he flew into Vancouver, then rented a car," Andi mused. "That makes no sense. Calgary's no farther away than Vancouver; he could have just driven from there."

"That does seem odd," Mac agreed. "Unless he had other business in Vancouver and came up here as a side trip."

"It looks like our victim was meeting someone at the pub." Eli held up a note he'd found on the table near the phone. "It says 'pub eight p.m.'"

"What time was the body found?" Alyson asked.

"Around nine o'clock," Andi answered.

"The guy was almost completely covered with snow when the couple found him. He couldn't have been at the pub very long," Trevor pointed out.

"It was snowing pretty hard, around eight inches an hour, but he still would have had to have been lying in the snow for at least thirty to forty minutes for it to cover him the way it did," Andi agreed.

"So maybe someone helped Mother Nature along," Eli concluded.

"You think someone buried him?" Mac asked.

"Either that or he never went to the pub and ended up in the snowbank prior to eight p.m."

"We should definitely check with the bartender," Alyson said. "Something isn't adding up."

"It might be a good idea to speak to the couple who found the body," Devon added. "Maybe we could get an idea of how much snow the body was actually buried under."

"Where does the bartender live?" Alyson asked.

"In an apartment over the pub." Andi looked at her watch. "It's a little early for Hank to be up and about. Maybe we should start with the couple."

"Do we know who they are?" Mac asked.

"No, but I can find out. Let's take a ride over to security headquarters. It's about a mile down the road so we should drive."

They headed back to the café to get the SUV and then drove to the security office. Even though the drive wasn't all that far it took almost ten minutes with the treacherous road conditions.

"Hey, Sheila," Andi greeted the young woman who sat behind the long counter that separated the lobby from the desk space when they arrived. "I'm showing a couple of guests around. This is Trevor Johnson and Alyson Prescott."

The others were waiting in the SUV.

"Nice to meet you. I hope you're enjoying your stay in spite of the weather." The pretty young woman shook each of their hands over the counter.

"We are, thank you. I don't suppose you have a bathroom?" Alyson asked. "Too much coffee at breakfast."

"Sure." Sheila buzzed the gate open. "Down the hall to your left."

Alyson walked down the hall and slipped through the second door on the right. Andi had told her that was where she'd find the records for all recent cases, including Bruce Long's. She looked around to make sure she was alone before quietly opening the file cabinet drawers. Each drawer was filled front to back with different colored folders, each folder labeled with a last name and a date.

Luckily, they were alphabetized: Langford, Littleton, Long. Alyson opened the last file and began to read. Bruce Long, found buried in a snowdrift at 8:57 p.m. by Rita and Mark Hawkins. The Hawkinses had reported seeing a human foot protruding from the snow pile as they walked back to their cabin after dinner. Resort security was called in to retrieve the body at 9:05. The victim appeared to have passed out on his way home from the pub. Official cause of death was hypothermia. Personal belongings included wallet, keys, military ring, and clothing, all being held in locker 712 until next of kin could be reached.

Alyson returned the file to the drawer and snuck back into the hall. She could hear Sheila laughing as Trevor told her a totally fictitious tale of the previous day's activities. Alyson considered using the facilities for real but decided she'd be pushing it timewise.

"What's so funny?" Alyson asked as she returned to the counter.

"Trevor was just filling us in on the mishap he had the last time he went skiing," Andi explained.

"Yeah, he's quite the storyteller." Alyson glanced at the clock. "Listen, we need to get going. I just realized how late it's getting. We're supposed to meet Devon and the others."

"Oh, right." Andi got up from the chair she had been sitting on. "We really should go. Have a good day." She waved to Sheila as they left.

"So did you find out anything?" Mac asked when Alyson, Trevor, and Andi returned to the vehicle.

"I got the names of the couple who found Long." Alyson slid into the front seat next to Devon. "Rita and Mark Hawkins. It didn't say where they were staying."

"Head over to reservations and I'll find out," Andi instructed.

"The file also listed his personal belongings." Alyson filled them in as Devon drove toward the main lodge. "Nothing out of the ordinary; still, it might not hurt to have a look. The notes said they're in locker 712."

"That's one of the lockers in the security office," Andi explained. "They're used mostly for lost-and-found items."

"How hard would it be to get a peek at locker 712?" Alyson asked.

"It might be tricky, but not impossible. We'd probably need a diversion."

"Oh, great. A diversion." Mac sighed. "I knew I wasn't off the hook completely. What's the plan?"

"Sheila's already seen us once today, so going back during her shift might be pushing our luck. The next shift change is at two o'clock. I know where the keys to the lockers are kept, so if someone can keep whoever's on duty busy, I'll sneak in and take a peak."

"A girl after my own heart." Trevor put his arm around Andi's shoulders. "Totally hot and an investigating mastermind."

Alyson looked in the rearview mirror. She noticed Andi smile at Trevor as they slowly made their way across the resort. Maybe there was a romance in the making after all.

"Here we are." Devon pulled up in front of the main lodge.

"Okay, you guys wait here and I'll get the Hawkinses' room number," Andi directed. "If they're staying at the lodge I'll wave to you and you can park and join me inside. Chances are, though, if they were walking from dinner or the pub to their lodging when they discovered the body, they're staying in one of the cabins."

Andi opened the door of the SUV and ran through the blizzard into the lobby. Someone had shoveled the steps, but there were already several inches of new snow on the flagstone walkway.

"It's a good thing we have four-wheel drive," Mac commented from the third-row seat. "The roads are getting pretty bad. I wonder why the plow hasn't been by for a while."

"I heard someone say that most of the snow removal team is working on trying to clear the slide," Eli filled her in. "I think there's only a skeleton crew left to take care of things around here."

"Well, I for one am all for getting the road cleared. It's kind of freaking me out to know there's no way out of here. I mean, what if there were a real emergency?"

"I wouldn't worry, Mac." Alyson tried to console her friend. "I'm sure the resort is prepared for whatever might come up."

"Like a psycho serial killer?"

"I doubt that's what we're dealing with." Alyson turned the heater up in an attempt to defrost the windows. "But if we are, I doubt he'd target us."

"Oh, no. We're just the ones snooping around, trying to uncover his plan."

"If you're not comfortable being part of this you can wait for us back at the house," Alyson offered.

"No, I'm fine. I've just always had this fear of being trapped. Knowing there's no way out is giving me a kind of claustrophobia. But I'm in. I'll be okay."

Andi slid into the seat next to Trevor. "I got the Hawkinses' cabin number. They're staying at the cabin two doors down from where Bruce Long was staying."

"Okay, let's check it out," Alyson said.

The drive to the cabin was a short one, less than a mile. But with the drifting snow and lack of visibility, the trip took several minutes.

"Cabin's dark," Devon commented. "Maybe they're out."

"They could be anywhere." Alyson tried to peer through the window, which had fogged up on the inside. "We'll have to come back later."

"So what now?" Devon asked.

"It's too early to meet with the bartender and the shift change at the security office won't be for several more hours. Maybe we should check out the maintenance shop," Mac suggested. "If Mario's burns were something other than an accident maybe we can find a clue."

"Sounds like a plan." Devon pulled out onto the snow-covered road. "Things are getting bad. We may have to lay low until a plow comes through. Even with four-wheel drive the drifting snow is causing some really deep sections of road."

"Let's see if we can get an ETA on the road crew while we're at maintenance. In fact, that might be a good cover for why we're even there," Andi said.

Once they arrived at the maintenance station, Devon found a place to park and they all piled out. The roads might not all have been cleared, but it looked as if the crew had plowed the parking lot at the maintenance facility at some point.

"Hey, Andi. What's up?" A man in a blue uniform greeted her as they made their way into the large warehouse that was used to repair equipment and store maintenance supplies.

"Hey, Charlie. I was out with my friends and noticed that the roads are getting really bad. Any idea when we can expect a plow to come through?"

"Most of the crew is helping out with the slide, but Bret Robbins stayed behind to take care of the village. I don't know where he is, though. He's not answering his radio. I've been trying to contact him for over an hour."

"Maybe the storm's interfering with the signal," Andi guessed.

"Maybe, but I've been able to reach everyone else all right. I'm betting he's home napping. I was thinking of heading over to his cabin to check it out. Now that Mario's gone the boss left me in charge. I want to do a good job."

"Speaking of Mario, I was wondering if you saw anything on the day of the accident."

Charlie shook his head. "I went home early; case of food poisoning. It was bad, stuff coming out from both ends. Mario was covering for me. He wasn't even supposed to be on shift that day. I can't tell you how bad I felt when I heard about the explosion."

"Do you happen to know how you got the food poisoning?" Andi asked.

"Must have been the roast beef sandwich I had for lunch. I was fine until I ate it."

"Where did you get it?" Andi pressed.

"Had it delivered from the staff cafeteria. It's been real busy the past few weeks with the resort being so crowded, so I decided to work while I ate."

"And you started feeling sick immediately after you ate?" Andi confirmed.

"Yeah. I called Mario and he came in to cover for me. I guess if it weren't for that sandwich I'd be the one in the hospital. I've really got to go check on Bret. It's important to me to do a good job, for Mario. He'd be having a coronary if he were here and the roads weren't plowed."

"Sure, go ahead. I'll talk to you later," Andi said, excusing him.

"Is there any way we can get a look at Mario's personnel file?" Alyson asked Andi.

"Yeah, later. After the human resources department closes. We could sneak in after dinner."

"It might be worth taking a peek. I doubt we'll find anything, but at this point we shouldn't leave any stone unturned," Alyson decided.

"HR is in the main lodge. We could have dinner there and then sneak over to the office after closing. I'll have Tony save us a table by the window and I'll ask Cookie to prepare us something special. He's the head chef for the resort. He can coax ordinary food into tasting like manna from heaven. He's an absolute genius in the kitchen. He's also quite a character. I'll introduce you. Say around eight?"

"Sounds good. Is there a specific dress code we should keep in mind?" Alyson asked.

"Not really. We're pretty casual around here. People usually dress sort of dressy casual in the lodge, but there's no real rule. I'm sure whatever you decide on will be fine."

"So what now?" Devon asked. "Should we look around to see if we can find anything related to the explosion?"

"Might as well. I wouldn't risk waking Hank up for at least another hour. He's the nicest guy in the world, but wake him up before he's ready and you're taking your life in your own hands. I should know; I tried it when I was eight. Scared the living daylights out of me. Since then I've never come a knocking until at least noon."

"It sounds like Hank's worked here for a long time," Mac commented as they sorted through drawers and cabinets.

"Since before I was born. Quite a few of the staff have been here since the early days with my grandfather."

"How about Mario?" Alyson asked as she opened and closed cabinet doors.

"He's only been here about five years. The supervisor before him had been here more than twenty years, though. As I've said, we're like a family here. Most people come for the season but end up staying for a lifetime."

"I think I found some kind of log." Eli held up a notebook. "It looks like it's used to track calls. There's a space for the time and date and for who called in the repair. There's also a space for recording whether the problem was fixed or needed further attention."

"Is Mario's last call logged in?" Mac asked.

"Yeah, December 25th, three twenty-eight p.m. Someone named Morgan called in to report that guests were complaining that the indoor pool was cold. That's all it says."

"Morgan is a concierge. If the water in the pool was cold she'd be the one the guests would talk to. The propane tank that exploded was the one used to heat the pool."

"If there was someone targeting Mario it all makes sense," Mac said. "Someone poisoned Charlie's sandwich so he had to go home and Mario was called in. Then whoever it was tampered with the propane tank so that the pool went cold. He could have set up the explosion at that point. Once Mario responded to the customer complaints, he did something that set off the explosion. Maybe simply turning the tank back on was the trigger. The would-be murderer could be long gone by then. Any evidence that may have existed— fingerprints or a detonator— were destroyed in the explosion."

"So how do we, a, find the killer, and b, prove our theory?" Andi asked.

"I'm not sure. I guess we just keep looking and hope we find something. It's too bad we've had so much snow. An investigation of the crime scene might prove helpful."

"The snow removal crew keep the propane tanks dug out religiously, but because that particular tank technically no longer exists, I doubt they've bothered."

"How about the pool?" Eli asked. "How have they heated it since the accident?"

"They haven't. The explosion happened on Christmas. A new tank was supposed to be delivered the next day, but the storm hit and it never arrived. There's another pool at Moose Lake Lodge; guests have been directed there."

"It's almost noon. Maybe we should get some lunch, then look up the friendly bartender," Alyson suggested.

"Yeah. I doubt we'll find anything else here," Devon agreed.

"There's a sub shop in town. They have sandwiches, soups, and salads," Andi told them. "You'll want to leave room for Cookie's dinner. Trust me; you'll be glad you did."

Chapter 5

After lunch they headed over to the pub. It was an old-fashioned-looking building with a wooden walkway and double doors. A large picture window revealed a plank floor and dozens of tables surrounded by wooden chairs. The bar ran the entire length of the building and was fashioned out of milled rough lumber made smooth by a thick varnish.

Andi looked through the window. "Oh, good. Hank's already downstairs." Tapping on the clear glass, she waved to the man inside.

"Hey, Andi. What's up?" An elderly man with a long gray beard and hair that reached halfway down his back asked after opening the door.

"I'm giving my friends a tour of the resort. I wanted to show them the pub and introduce them to Grizzly Mountain's orneriest resident. Can we come in?"

"Sure, why not? You all look a little young for afternoon cocktails, however."

"We're not here to drink," Alyson corrected the rugged mountain man. "We just arrived yesterday in the middle of the man-in-the-snowbank crisis. I guess we were just curious. One of the security personnel told us he was in here before he ended up in the snow. Do you remember seeing him?"

"Yeah, he was here. Came in around eight. Ordered a forty-year-old bottle of single malt scotch. I didn't even know we had such a thing. Someone must have special-ordered it. It's a lot pricier than most people want."

"He ordered the whole bottle?" Alyson asked.

"Said he had some friends coming. Mentioned some type of reunion."

"Did anyone show up?"

"No. He took the bottle over to that table in the corner and had one drink. Next thing I know, he's staggering out of here. Left the rest of the bottle on the table. No one ever did show up to drink the rest."

"Do you still have it?"

"I put it behind the bar. Figured the guy paid for it, maybe he'd be back for it when he sobered up. When I found out he was dead I credited his charge card and put the bottle back into inventory."

"Do you think it's odd that the guy was staggering after only one drink?'

"Some people are lightweights. That stuff is strong. Figured he could have been drinking before he wandered in here and the scotch put him over the top."

"I'd like to buy the rest of the bottle." Alyson whipped out her credit card. "I'm not going to drink it. It's a gift for my dad."

"I don't know. You're underage."

"Come on, Hank," Andi pleaded. "We won't tell and we won't drink it, I promise. Alyson told me earlier that she was looking for the perfect gift for her dad. It's his fortieth birthday. A forty-year-old bottle of scotch would be perfect."

"It has been opened," Hank reminded them.

"My dad won't care about that," Alyson assured him.

"Well, okay. But if anyone asks, I know nothing about this transaction."

"What transaction?" Andi bagged the scotch as Hank ran Alyson's card.

"I know you didn't really buy the scotch for your dad. So what's with the expensive souvenir?" Mac asked Alyson after they left the bar.

"Evidence. The whole thing is just too odd. Think about it: Bruce Long went into a bar and ordered an expensive bottle of scotch the bartender doesn't even know he had. He told the bartender he was going to meet some friends who never showed up, had one drink, and ended up dead in a snowbank."

"You think the scotch was drugged," Devon guessed.

"Bingo. Furthermore, I think someone planted the scotch, either because they knew it was the victim's preference, or they somehow instructed the victim to buy that particular brand and year."

"So who planted the scotch and what happened to the friends he was supposed to be meeting?" Eli asked.

"Both good questions. But is there a way we can test this scotch for drugs?" Alyson asked Andi.

"Dr. Mark might have a way, but I don't know how we'd get him to test it without telling him why we want it done."

"Do you do pre-employment drug testing?" Mac asked.

"Yeah, and random tests on all safety-sensitive personnel."

"Are the tests done locally?"

"They're sent over to the lab."

"So all we need to do is break in again and find a drug kit. I can do the test. It's really pretty easy. We can test the victim's blood while we're at it."

"Blood?" Andi asked. "How are you going to get his blood?"

"We'll have to draw it. It'll be hard on someone who's been dead for twenty-four hours but not impossible."

"Are you thinking of performing this procedure before or after we indulge in Cookie's epicurean delights?" Eli asked.

"After," Mac answered. "We want to be sure no one is around. The later the better."

Andi turned pale. "Okay, but if my dinner ends up on Dr. Mark's floor don't say I didn't warn you."

"You can wait in the hall or in one of the other rooms. I'll really only need one person to help me after we find the kits."

"I'll do it," Eli volunteered. "Where my woman goes, I go."

"Your woman?" Mac asked.

"A little too chauvinistic?"

"A lot too chauvinistic. But you can help anyway."

"It's almost two o'clock. We can head over to the security offices if you want," Andi interrupted.

"Okay, let's go." Alyson nodded. "The more we investigate these so-called accidents, the more convinced I am they weren't."

They once again piled into the SUV and headed across the resort. Alyson had yet to get a glimpse of the ski lifts with all the snow, but the town was delightful. The resort had been built to provide an atmosphere that was both woodsy and charming. Many of the businesses had themes, such as the fifties diner.

"So everyone is clear on the plan?" Alyson asked the rest of them once they arrived at the security office.

"We're clear." Devon turned the tires into the nearest snowbank. "We'll be close by if you get into trouble."

Alyson walked into the security office, where a young uniformed officer sat behind the desk.

"Can I help you, ma'am?"

Alyson shook the snow off her jacket and pushed back the hood, revealing her face and hair. "I seem to have gotten my vehicle stuck in a snowbank. It's right out in front of your office. I was hoping you could help me get it out."

"Sure thing." The young man grabbed his coat and gloves and headed out into the blizzard with Alyson on his heels.

"Doesn't look too bad." The man opened the driver's side door. "I'll push while you give it gas."

From the corner of her eye she could see Andi sneak in the front door of the security office.

"Are you the only one here?" Alyson asked. "In case we can't get it out ourselves."

"I'm here alone, but I think we can manage this. When I tell you to, put the vehicle in reverse and give it a little gas. Not too much or we'll only bury it deeper."

Alyson hadn't seen Andi come out yet, so she tried to stall. "When you say a little gas how much is a little? Half a throttle?"

"Less than that. Just a gentle pressure on the gas pedal should do it." The man got into position. "Okay, give it gas."

Alyson gave the vehicle too much, causing the wheels to spin.

"Not that much," the patient security guard instructed. "Just a tap. I'll push and you steer."

Alyson saw Andi sneak out and run toward the snowbank where the others were hiding. She gave the vehicle just a tap of gas and gently drove it out of the snow.

"Thanks so much." Alyson shook the man's hand. "I never would have gotten it free without your help."

"My pleasure. Have a nice day now, and watch your speed. The roads can be treacherous during storms. I wouldn't want to see you have a more serious accident."

"I'll be careful. Thanks again."

Alyson drove down the road to where the others were hiding. Alyson slid into the passenger seat, relinquishing the driver's seat to Devon.

"So what'd you find?" Alyson asked after everyone was inside.

"The locker had the man's clothes, a set of keys, a military ring—marines, I think—and a wallet. His wallet had several credit cards, a driver's license, and a few random photos. There was also a note that had the brand and year of the scotch he ordered in the bar on it."

"If it was his favorite brand he wouldn't have had to write it down," Devon concluded. "Someone must have told him to order it."

"Yeah, but who? And why?" Eli asked.

"If we figure that out we may find the murderer," Alyson said.

"It's after three. Maybe we should swing by the Hawkins cabin, then head home to rest and clean up for dinner," Devon suggested. "I have a feeling this is going to be a late night."

"Good idea," Alyson agreed. "Personally, I'm freezing. A nice long soak in that Jacuzzi tub would be heaven."

The Hawkinses were still out, so they dropped Andi off at her house and arranged to pick her up for dinner at a quarter to eight.

Chapter 6

The Grizzly Mountain Lodge was about as perfect a ski lodge as you could find. A large main room with a vaulted ceiling was made to feel cozy and intimate by the huge fireplace taking up one entire wall. The fireplace opening was so large that a fully grown man could stand in its center. The room was furnished with comfortable forest green sofas, large wooden tables, and floor-to-ceiling bookshelves that invited weary skiers to curl up by the fire with a current best seller or an age-old classic. The most striking feature of the room, though, was that one entire wall was encased in glass, which, in daylight, provided a breathtaking view of the frozen lake and the towering mountains in the distance.

"Wow, this place is really spectacular," Mac murmured as they wandered through the common room to the restaurant, which boasted its own wall of windows with a view similar to the one found in the other area. The difference here was that many of the windows were actually glass doors that opened onto a large deck where outdoor dining was possible in the summer.

In the center of the room was a baby grand piano at which an excellent pianist played holiday tunes and requests.

The host greeted them. "I've got a table reserved by the window. The best in the house."

"Thanks, Tony. Come on; I'll introduce you to Cookie before we sit down. He's preparing a meal especially for us."

Andi led them through the huge kitchen, past walk-in refrigerators, floor-to-ceiling glass-fronted cabinets, and huge gas stoves. Thousands of dollars' worth of steaks and freshly grilled seafood covered almost every surface as an army of cooks prepared dinners for the hundred or so guests in the restaurant.

"Cookie, these are the friends I was telling you about. This is Alyson, Trevor, and Mac. I think you might have already met Devon and Eli. They've been here a while."

"Glad to meet you." Alyson held out her hand and tried not to let her mouth hang open in surprise. Cookie was a huge man; at least two hundred and fifty pounds, probably more. He was tattooed from head to toe and looked like he had just stepped off the battlefield of some great war. Two of his teeth were missing and his head was shaved bald.

"Bit skinny. Cookie will fix you right up," Cookie promised.

"Uh, thanks," Alyson responded as Cookie ignored her hand and instead gave her a great big bear hug that nearly cracked her ribs.

"We'll be out front," Andi informed him. "Table twelve." She grabbed Alyson's hand and led the rest out of the kitchen to the reserved table.

"Wow, he's really..." Alyson searched for the right word. "Something. How'd he ever come to work here?"

"He was in the war with my grandfather. Afterward he came back here and has been tantalizing our guests' taste buds ever since. I know he looks rough, but he's really a teddy bear, and he can cook like you've never tasted. Whatever he comes up with for dinner will be the best food you've ever eaten. If I didn't burn tons of calories skiing all day I'd weigh five hundred pounds."

"You have a lot of interesting employees here," Alyson observed. "I like that. It shows the place has character."

"Dinner was everything you promised." Alyson groaned and placed her palm over her stomach as they waddled out of the restaurant a couple of hours later. "I doubt I'll have to eat again the whole time I'm here."

"Don't count on it. Fresh mountain air tends to stimulate the appetite. So where to first? The lab or the human resources office?"

"The HR office definitely," Mac said.

The office was located down a hallway that housed most of the other administrative offices at the resort. They were all deserted with the exception of a cleaning crew that was three doors down from human resources.

Andi unlocked the door and they all slipped inside. She pulled the blinds and turned on the light. "We'll need to hurry. The cleaning crew could be by at any time. The personnel files are in that long file cabinet along the back wall. The key should be," she opened a desk drawer, "right here."

Andi hurried over to the cabinet and opened the top drawer. She sorted through the file until she found the one labeled Mario Gonzales.

"He was hired five years ago, which I knew. Married, no children, which I also knew. Previous to his employment here, he served a tour of duty in Afghanistan. It doesn't look like there's anything unusual. It's a pretty standard education and employment history." Andi paused. "That's interesting."

"What?" Mac asked.

"Prior to enlisting in the marines, Mario was in medical school. He never mentioned anything that would lead me to believe he'd trained to be a doctor."

"So why was he working here as a maintenance man?" Alyson wondered.

"I have no idea." Andi returned the file to the drawer.

"It's odd for a man with that level of education to take such a menial job," Mac commented.

"I agree, although Mario's job can be pretty complex. There's a lot of pretty sophisticated equipment that needs to be maintained. Still, it is odd." Andi shrugged. "We'd better go. I hear the cleaning staff next door. This office will be next."

Andi and the others snuck back into the hallway and out to the main lobby.

"You said Mario's sister also works here?" Alyson whispered.

"Carmen. She works in the cantina."

"Do you think she'd talk to us? Maybe she knows why Mario was a maintenance worker rather than a doctor."

"I guess we could try. It's late now, though. Maybe tomorrow."

"Try to set it up. For now, let's head over to the clinic," Alyson said.

As it was the previous evening, the clinic was dark and deserted. They made their way to the lab before turning on any lights.

"You guys look around for the drug test kits; Eli and I will get the blood sample," Mac instructed as she picked up a syringe and a vial and headed back into the dark hallway.

"Okay, if you were drug test kits where would you be?" Alyson mumbled as she began to sort through drawers and cabinets.

"Do you think this is really going to work?" Trevor asked. "Don't those kits just test for specific types of drugs? What if this drug is something else?"

"Honestly, I'm not an expert on drug testing, but it's worth a try," Alyson answered.

"If we do prove that the scotch was spiked with some type of drug, then what?" Andi asked.

"I guess we'll have to tell someone at that point. If Bruce Long was murdered we need to be sure the proper authorities are called in," Alyson responded.

"Only problem is, in this storm no one, even the cops, are getting anywhere near the resort. I guess our security patrol could do an investigation, though."

"I think I hear sirens." Devon stopped rummaging through the cabinet he had been searching through and listened.

"We need to get out of here." Andi slammed the drawer she had been looking through. "That's the siren from our ambulance. I'm betting we're going to have company at any moment."

Andi and the others headed into the hallway. Mac and Eli were headed toward them. They all hurried out the front door, being careful to lock it behind them.

"Did you get the sample?" Alyson asked Mac.

"We did. Did you get the test kits?" Mac asked Alyson.

"No, we heard the siren before we could find them."

"It looks like the emergency lights are coming from the main lodge," Andi said. "Let's go check it out."

When they arrived the emergency medical crew was loading a body into the back of the ambulance. Andi's Aunt Veronica was speaking to one of the medical technicians.

"What happened?" Alyson followed Andi as she rushed over to her aunt.

"Oh, Andi. One of the guests appears to have had a heart attack. I'm afraid we were too late. She was alone in her room. We wouldn't even know about it except for the fact that she appears to have been running a bath when the heart attack occurred. The tub ran over and the water leaked down to the room below. The occupants called the desk to report the leak and we found the woman dead on the floor."

"Oh, God. That's awful. Is there anything I can do to help?"

"Actually, can you see if you can find a new room for the occupants of 312? I asked Dawn to do it, but with all the commotion she's pretty swamped with curious guests."

"Sure, no problem."

Alyson whispered, "Any way we could get a look at the woman's room?"

"She was in 412. I can get you a key, but you'll have to hurry. I'm sure housekeeping will be up there shortly to clean up the water damage."

Andi slipped behind the desk, telling the clerk she'd take care of finding a room for the guests in room 312. She slipped

Alyson a key to 412, telling her that she'd ring the room on the intraresort phone if she saw housekeeping heading that way.

"What exactly are we looking for?" Mac asked after they'd made their way into the room.

"I don't know. Anything unusual," Alyson answered.

"I found her wallet." Devon pulled it from the woman's purse. "Her name was Stacy King She was only twenty-nine. A bit young for a heart attack."

"Twenty-nine? Really?" Alyson asked. "I wonder why they're assuming a heart attack. That seems unlikely."

"Probably due to lack of any other obvious cause," Mac concluded. "We can assume she didn't have any obvious bruising or contusions."

"There's an invitation in her purse," Devon added.

"An invitation to what?" Mac asked.

"Here, actually. There's a note that says, 'Hi, old friend. Join me for New Year's at the resort; my treat, of course. We'll catch up on old times.'"

"It's not signed?" Mac asked.

"Afraid not."

"That's odd." Alyson crossed the room and took the note from Devon.

"You know what else is odd? The woman was getting ready to take a bath, but there are two wineglasses on the coffee table. Both half full," Mac pointed.

"So where's the friend?" Eli asked.

The phone on the bedside table buzzed.

"We'd better go." Alyson stuck the note into her pocket.

They snuck out and headed toward the elevator. The housekeeping crew was just getting out of the elevator as they got in.

"That was close," Mac breathed. "Another few seconds and they would have seen us coming out of the room."

"I wonder if Andi can find out who paid for the woman's room," Devon said.

As soon as the elevator reached the lobby, Alyson hurried over to the desk. "Andi, can you find out who paid for room 312?"

"Sure, hang on." Andi pulled up the woman's registration information. "It says the room was paid for with an employee comp."

"An employee comp?" Alyson asked.

"Yeah, employees can earn complimentary nights at the resort for doing things like working overtime or perfect attendance. It's our way of rewarding employees for going above and beyond. Additionally, every employee gets comp nights on their work anniversary, depending on their years of service. Most employees use the comps to have friends or relatives visit."

"Does it say whose employee comps were used?"

"No, I'm afraid not."

"So who would know?" Alyson asked.

"Whoever made the reservation. They would have had to confirm the comp nights with HR."

"Can you find out who made the reservation?"

"I guess I could check with HR to see who cashed in comp nights for this week. The problem is going to be coming up with a plausible reason why I want that information. I don't really want my dad to find out what we're doing."

"Let's head back over to our place to compare notes," Alyson suggested. "I feel like I see a pattern emerging, but to be honest, I have no idea what it is. I think a little brainstorming might be in order."

"Sure, just let me finish moving 312. I'll meet you at the Expedition."

After Andi finished helping out they all headed back to the house where they were staying.

"Is your dad here?" Mac asked as they pulled up in the front of the house.

"His car's here. The place is dark, so he's probably already in bed," Eli answered.

"You guys get comfortable in the living room," Devon volunteered. "I'll check. Just keep it down. If he's asleep we want him to stay that way."

Mac and Eli settled onto one of the three couches facing the fireplace, Trevor and Andi on another, with Alyson on the third.

"Fires still burning," Eli observed. "If Dad did go to bed it couldn't have been too long ago. Can I get anyone something to eat or drink?"

"I'm still stuffed from dinner, but a soda would be nice," Mac answered.

"Anyone else?"

The others nodded in agreement.

Eli went into the kitchen just as Devon returned to the room.

"Dad's watching a movie in our room, but he said he'd lay low. He's not one to interfere in what I'm sure he imagines is some teenage make-out session, so we should be fine. Let's just keep it quiet. Where's Eli?"

"Getting sodas." Alyson snuggled up next to Devon.

"So where do we start?" Devon put his arm around her shoulders.

"I'm not sure really. I just figure three deaths—or almost deaths, in Mario's case—in three days. Seems beyond coincidence. If you look at each event in isolation it seems like a believable accident, but if you look at them as a whole it seems like something more. Add to that the fact that the woman was in the room alone, supposedly getting ready to take a bath, but there were two wineglasses on the coffee table, both half full. I guess it's not unheard of for someone to leave without finishing their drink, but it almost looked like the encounter was interrupted."

"You think one of the drinks was drugged?" Andi concluded.

"It would explain why a twenty-nine-year-old woman appears to have had a heart attack."

"The woman was running a bath when she fell unconscious," Mac pointed out. "Do you think there are drugs that can cause a heart attack so quickly? If she wasn't feeling well prior to the attack she would have turned off the water in the tub."

"I'm no expert on drugs," Alyson said, "but I'm guessing there are."

"Do you think we should bring our suspicions to someone else?" Trevor asked. "Like maybe Dr. Mark or the security patrol?"

"If we do we'll have to admit we've been sneaking around, and without some type of actual evidence to distract them from that fact, I'll probably just end up spending the rest of the week in my room," Andi pointed out.

"We wouldn't want that." Trevor put his arm around Andi.

"If we get something really concrete I'll go to my dad and take my chances. If we're wrong and we're seeing murder where there's only bad luck, I'd just as soon stay out of the dog house."

"I wonder if there's any connection between Bruce Long and Stacy King," Mac mused. "If they were both poisoned, I'm thinking we may have a serial killer on our hands."

"Someone may just be killing randomly," Trevor pointed out. "Maybe there's no connection between the victims."

"That's what I'm afraid of," Mac informed him. "A killer with a specific motive is one thing; someone who kills for no apparent reason is another. With the road closed off, someone who's killing randomly would have an unlimited number of potential victims."

"I hadn't thought of that. Maybe I should bring our suspicions to my dad after all," Andi realized.

"Let's see what we can find out tomorrow, then decide," Mac suggested. "So far we have tons of speculation but no proof. The possibility that these really are isolated accidents still exists."

"Okay, so what's the plan for tomorrow?" Trevor asked.

"We can go see Carmen," Alyson said. "Maybe she can give us some insight into Mario's past that might make him a victim."

"And tomorrow night we can take another pass at finding the drug tests," Eli added.

"And I'll check with HR to see whose employee comp was used this week," Andi volunteered. "I'll just need to figure out a logical reason for inquiring."

"Has anyone heard an update on the weather?" Mac asked. "I'd love to have an hour or two on the Net. The more we know about each of the victims, the better chance we have of finding a link between them."

"I'll see if I can find out," Andi promised. "My dad usually keeps pretty good track of the weather. I know the guests are getting restless. We weren't able to run the lifts at all today."

"It seems like it isn't snowing as hard as it has been." Devon walked over to the large picture window. "And the winds have died down considerably. Maybe it won't be so bad tomorrow."

"I hope you're right. We can run the lifts in the snow. It's the wind that's the problem. Guests tend to get cranky if they miss more than one day on the slopes."

Alyson yawned. "I guess we should plan to get together in the morning. Not too early, though. All this sleuthing is making me tired."

"I'll bring pastries if you can make the coffee," Andi volunteered.

"You need a ride?" Trevor asked.

"No, I can always get a ride around here. Say we meet at nine?"

"Sounds good," Trevor answered for them all.

"Something just occurred to me." Devon sat down next to Alyson. "Both Bruce Long and Stacy King were here alone. Is it common for guests to come to the resort by themselves?"

"Not usually," Andi answered. "Bruce Long was supposed to meet someone and Stacy King obviously knows an employee, so I guess it's not really all that strange that they had single rooms."

"I sure would like to know who Bruce Long was supposed to meet." Alyson rested her head on Devon's shoulder.

"You said the phones in the rooms are for intraresort use. Is there any way to find out who may have called Bruce Long's room on the night of his death?" Alyson asked Andi.

"I'm not sure. If guests know the extension they want they can dial directly without going through the switchboard. Still, I guess there could be a computer record. I'm afraid technical stuff isn't my area of expertise."

"I'll check into it," Devon said. "Can you get me access to the main server?"

"I don't know. What's a main server?"

"I'll see if I can subtly get the info I need from my dad. We often discuss jobs; he shouldn't find it strange I'm asking about this one."

"Okay, good. Sorry I couldn't be more help."

"Don't worry, you've been a lot of help. There's no way we'd be able to investigate this without you. You're part of the team." Trevor squeezed Andi's shoulder.

"I really should get home. My dad starts to worry around this time."

Trevor stood up. "I'll take you." He turned to Devon. "Can I borrow the Expedition?"

"Sure." Devon threw him the keys.

"I'll see everyone tomorrow." Andi got up and started toward the door.

"Don't wait up." Trevor winked as he followed Andi out into the storm.

"I hope Andi knows what she's getting herself into." Mac chuckled as Trevor closed the door behind him.

"I think Andi can take care of herself." Alyson stood up and stretched. "I'm going to bed. See you all in the morning."

"I think I'll head up too." Devon followed Alyson up the stairs.

"Alone at last." Alyson heard Eli say as he turned off the overhead lights.

Chapter 7

As promised, Andi showed up the next morning with a bag from the resort bakery. The wind had all but stopped and the snow had slowed to a gentle dusting. Although the drifts were so high you couldn't see beyond the snowbank directly in front of you, it really was beautiful.

"The lifts are open today." Andi set the bag of goodies on the table. "Maybe if we get done playing Nancy Drew early enough we can get a couple of runs in. With all this fresh powder the skiing should be awesome."

"Sounds good. Is the Internet back up?" Mac asked.

"Not yet, but it should be by this afternoon. There's actually supposed to be a partial clearing around two. My dad said that helicopters from Vancouver are coming in to retrieve the two bodies. I guess it's a good thing you were able to get the blood sample last night."

"Are the police going to conduct any type of investigation?" Devon asked.

"I'm not sure, but I sort of doubt it. Everyone still thinks the things that happened were accidents. Unfortunately, the killer, if there is one, has done a good job of making everything look perfectly natural."

"Did you get hold of Carmen?" Alyson poured herself a cup of coffee and took a sugar doughnut from the bag.

"Not yet," Andi answered. "I didn't want to call too early. I'll try now."

"I talked to Dad," Devon said while Andi made her call. "He said the phone system is run by a centralized computer. We should be able to access phone records for the dates in question if we can get inside the room that houses the server."

"Did he say where it is?" Eli asked.

"The room that houses all the mainframes for the resort is in the admin wing of the main lodge."

Alyson looked behind her as Andi approached from the hallway.

"Carmen's going to catch a ride into Vancouver with the helicopter when they get here, but she said we could come by to see her this morning. I told her we'd be there in about an hour."

"Has she heard any more about Mario's condition?" Mac asked.

Andi shook her head. "With the phones down she's been as isolated as the rest of us. I think that's why she's flying in to see him."

"Any idea when the satellite phones will be back up?" Devon asked.

"I'm guessing this afternoon if the weather holds, as is predicted. My dad said there's another front coming in behind this one, so the reprieve may be short-lived. If we do get Internet service we should take advantage of it."

"I need to call my mom too," Mac informed them. "I told her I'd call to check in. I had no idea there'd be no phone service."

"We usually only lose service for an entire day maybe ten days out of the year. You guys just picked an extrastormy week to be here. The weather forecast is for a series of storms, one right after the other."

"Did you mention to Carmen why we wanted to talk to her?" Mac helped herself to a second cream-filled doughnut.

"I just said we needed to ask her a few questions. She didn't ask about what and I didn't volunteer. We should decide how much we want to tell her."

"As little as possible," Alyson said. "We don't want to worry her. Although I don't know how we're going to casually ask her about Mario's past without letting her in on the idea that we suspect foul play."

"I could go alone under the guise of dropping off a get-well gift for Mario. I could subtly work in the whole medical school thing," Andi suggested. "It might be less intimidating than if we all showed up."

"That's a good idea," Mac agreed. "Don't you think so, guys?"

"Yeah, it makes a lot of sense." Devon nodded. "Trevor can drive you. Meet us back here after you talk to her."

"We should go now. I'll need to stop off in the village to get a gift."

"Are you feeling okay?" Mac asked Alyson after Andi left. "You look a little pale."

"I'm fine. I guess I'm just tired."

"I hope you're not getting sick."

"I doubt it. I think I'm just having a hard time getting started this morning."

"Yesterday was a long day and we did spend half of it soaking wet," Devon pointed out.

"I'm fine, really. I'm going to run upstairs to get dressed."

Alyson and the others were sitting in front of the fire discussing the advantages of different types of skis when Trevor and Andi returned.

"What'd you find out?" Alyson poured fresh cups of coffee all around.

"We asked Carmen about the whole doctor thing," Andi started. "I told her that Mario had mentioned to me one time that he went to medical school and I had always wondered what happened. She said he'd wanted to be a doctor ever since he was a little boy. They came from a poor family, so there was really no way he could afford medical school until he found out about a government program in which the military would pay for school in exchange for several years of service after his residency. Mario's a real pacifist, not at all the military type, but at the time Canada was at peace and had been for some time, so he saw it as his opportunity to make his dream come true."

"And then 9/11 happened," Alyson guessed.

"Exactly. By the time he finished his residency and was ready to fulfill his obligation to the marines we were smack dab in the middle of the Afghan War. He was deployed overseas almost immediately. Carmen doesn't know what happened there, but when he came home he was a different person. He heard about the maintenance position from a friend and he's been here ever since."

"And Carmen? How did she come to work here too?" Devon asked.

"She came up one summer to visit Mario and fell in love with the place. She applied for the position at the cantina and has been here ever since as well."

"Mario's employee file said he was married. Do you know if that happened before or after he got here?" Mac asked.

"During his residency Mario fell in love with one of the nurses. When he went off to war he asked her to wait for him, but when he got home from the war he pretty much turned his back on everyone. He came here and stopped communicating with anyone from his previous life. First Carmen followed him and then Jessica. Jessica applied to be a nurse at the clinic. Carmen said Jessica knew what she wanted and she wanted Mario. She refused to let him wallow in whatever self-pity had brought him here. She finally married Mario last summer."

"Wow, talk about true love. Mario must be a pretty special guy to command such loyalty," Alyson observed.

"Yeah, he's a sweetie."

"You said Mario was in the marines. Bruce Long had a ring from the marines. Maybe that's the link," Alyson speculated.

"Could be," Devon agreed.

"You think someone is killing marines?" Trevor asked.

"Maybe. Or maybe just specific marines," Alyson guessed. "Like maybe Afghan vets."

"If the Internet ever comes back up we should be able to find out where and when Bruce Long served," Mac said. "It might help us figure out exactly what happened to Mario. Is there anyone else Mario was close to? Anyone he might have confided in?"

"He was close to Charlie. I guess we could talk to him again," Andi suggested.

"Do you think he's working today?" Mac asked.

"Probably. With Mario out and so many people working on the snowslide, we're drastically understaffed."

"Let's go see if he's around." Alyson stood up immediately.

"Be sure to bundle up," Devon warned her.

"Don't worry, Dad, I will."

They once again climbed into the Expedition and headed to the maintenance yard. The sun was peeking through the clouds, making it appear as if there were millions of tiny diamonds on the fresh-fallen snow. It really was beautiful.

Charlie was just climbing into a snowplow when they arrived.

"Hey, Charlie. Plowing today?" Andi called.

"Yeah. Bret's still AWOL, so I'm trying to cover his job and mine. When I finally catch up with that guy I'm going to kill him."

"He's been missing since yesterday?" Andi asked.

"Yeah, but don't tell your dad. He's a bit of a slacker, but we're pretty good friends. I'd hate to see him get fired."

"Your secret's safe with me," Andi assured him. "Let me know if there's anything we can do to help."

"Any of you know how to drive a loader?"

"Sorry." Andi laughed. "If we run across Bret we'll send him in your direction."

"Thanks. I need to get going. They're opening the runs on the front side of the mountain today and the road to the lifts is a mess."

"Okay, see you later." Andi waved.

"You didn't ask him about Mario," Alyson pointed out.

"He was in a hurry. It would have seemed odd to make casual conversation. We can ask him later."

"Do you think it's strange that Bret has been missing since yesterday?" Mac asked after they returned to the SUV.

"I don't know. Charlie didn't seem that concerned," Andi pointed out.

"Yeah, but Charlie doesn't know about the other things that have been happening," Alyson reminded her.

"You think something happened to him?"

"Maybe. In light of everything else we know I wouldn't rule it out. Maybe we should check out his residence," Alyson suggested.

"Okay. Bret lives in one of the condos behind the main lodge that we use for employee housing. I'm not sure my passkey will work on his door, but we can try. Just take a left at the service road right before the main drive going up to the lodge," Andi instructed Devon.

The condos were mostly deserted at this time of day, when everyone was working. Bret's condo was the third from the left on the second floor. Andi's key turned the lock, but the door refused to budge.

"That's strange." Andi wiggled the doorknob. "It feels like the door is locked from the inside with a dead bolt."

"He must be in there," Alyson deduced. She tried looking through the window, but the curtains were drawn except for a narrow slit.

"Bret, are you in there?" Andi pounded on the door.

They waited for a minute, but no one answered, so Andi knocked again.

"You guys looking for Bret?" The next-door neighbor poked his head out of his door.

"Yeah, have you seen him?"

"He left early this morning. Might be working."

"Actually, he didn't show up at work today. If you see him can you tell him Charlie is looking for him?"

"Will do."

Alyson had a strange feeling as they turned and walked away. If Bret was out who had locked the door from the inside?

"If Bret left his apartment this morning but never showed up for work maybe he's playing hooky after all," Mac concluded.

"I guess," Andi agreed. "It's a pretty bad time to be AWOL. I'm not sure he deserves Charlie's loyalty."

"I had the feeling Charlie's loyalty had more to do with his friendship with Mario than Bret," Alyson said.

"Let's head over to HR to check on the comps," Andi suggested. "Then maybe we can get a couple of hours skiing in after lunch. With all this fresh powder the runs should be in excellent shape."

"I want to check the phone records," Devon reminded them. "Once I get into the server room it shouldn't take too long to access the mainframe."

"Okay, you check the phone records while Andi checks with HR; then we'll go over to the café for lunch," Alyson said.

"I'll go with Devon," Mac offered, "in case he needs some help."

"Okay. The rest of us will wait in the lobby," Alyson said. "We don't want to look too obvious."

Forty minutes later the gang was seated at a large booth in the café.

"Twelve employees used comps this week," Andi started. "I guess Christmas is a popular time to have friends and family visit."

"Did you get a list?" Alyson asked.

"Yes." Andi handed the list to Alyson. "I think you'll find number eight particularly interesting."

"Bret Robbins. Charlie's Bret?"

"One and the same."

"Does it say who he comped?"

"No, but I figured we should ask the other employees who they comped and we'll see if Bret sponsored Stacy King by process of elimination."

"How hard is it going to be to track the other eleven down?" Mac asked.

"Not hard. I know where they all work. In fact, two of them work right here: the cook and the hostess."

"Okay, let's ask," Alyson said.

"Order me a coffee if the waitress comes by," Andi told them.

"If Bret's comp wasn't Stacy maybe he's AWOL because he has a guest of the female persuasion visiting," Trevor speculated.

"I guess that could fit," Alyson agreed.

Andi returned to the table and sat down next to Trevor. "Two down, nine to go."

"How about the phone records?" Alyson asked.

"There were quite a few calls made on the twenty-sixth. Mac and I didn't have time to go through all of them so we made a hard copy. We'll look them over while we eat," Devon said.

"Okay, let's order. I'm starving," Trevor said. "I'm thinking ham and salami on a cheese roll."

"They have something called an Italian special," Andi informed him. "It has ham, salami, provolone, and Swiss, heated under the broiler, then topped off with lettuce, tomato, and onion."

"Sounds good. How's the potato salad?"

"It's good, but I prefer the pasta salad," Andi told Trevor. "The soup of the day is usually pretty good too."

"I'm thinking something light. Do they have salads?" Alyson asked.

"They have a spinach with hot bacon dressing that's really good. They also have a Cobb and a pretty good chef's salad."

The waitress came over to serve their drinks. She read off the specials of the day and informed them that today's soups were hearty tomato or Cajun shrimp chowder.

"So who else in on the list?" Alyson asked after they had placed their orders.

"Steve Brown and Randy Fallon, two lift operators. We can probably find both of them in the pub after the lifts close. Stella Gregson works in the deli. Carrie Brandywine and Karen Bates, who both work in housekeeping. As a matter of fact, Karen was one of the housekeepers who were sent to clean Stacy King's room last night, so we can ask her about that while we're at it."

"You think she'd tell us what she found in the room?" Mac asked.

"Probably. She's worked here a while, so we know each other pretty well."

"Who else is on the list?" Alyson asked.

"Dawn Regency, the desk clerk you met last night; Tim Smith, a waiter at the lodge; Tanya Ford, a hairdresser; and Charlie Epson, the maintenance guy you already met."

"So where should we start?" Alyson cut the tuna melt the waitress had convinced her to try.

"The deli is just a few doors over, so I suggest we start with Stella." Andi poured a puddle of ketchup on her plate. "Then we can head over to the lodge to talk to Dawn and see where Carrie and Karen are working today."

"Stella was working last night. Do you think she's here this afternoon?" Alyson salted her fries.

"I'm not sure. If not I know where she lives."

"You said there were a lot of intraresort calls on the twenty-sixth. Are they listed by room number?" Alyson asked Devon.

"Yeah, room number and time of call."

"So all we need to do is look for Bruce Long's cabin number," Alyson said. "Do you know what that might be?"

"It's C12." Andi answered

"Let's see. There was a call to C12 at four fifty-eight p.m. from the pub," Devon told them.

"That's not going to help us much. The lifts close at four o'clock, so the pub is usually packed by that time," Andi said.

"Whoever used the phone at the pub could have planted the scotch, especially if the bartender was extrabusy at the time," Eli observed.

"Are there any calls to or from room 412 in the lodge either on the twenty-sixth or -seventh?" Andi asked. "That would be Stacy King's room."

"There was a call from L412 to the beauty salon at nine twenty-three on the twenty-seventh," Devon reported.

"So I guess we should ask if she was in when we talk to Tanya," Alyson said. "Maybe Stacy told someone who she was meeting."

After they finished lunch they stopped off at the deli to learn that Stella had used her comps for her best friend. Tim Smith happened to be there, eating lunch with his parents, whom he had comped. Tanya Ford confirmed that she had indeed done

Stacy King's hair on the morning of the twenty-seventh, but she didn't know who the woman was meeting that evening. Tanya did say that Stacy had seemed nervous about it.

Next they headed over to the lodge. Luckily, the village was fairly compact and the distance between the various locations they had to visit was minimal.

"Hi, Dawn," Andi greeted her as they walked into the lobby. "I'm helping HR with a little recordkeeping. You used comp nights this week. I need to know who they were for."

"My sister and her daughter. I hadn't seen them in almost a year. I thought this would be a good time to have them out, but with all the extra shifts I've had to cover I've barely gotten to visit with them. At least they're opening the lifts on the front side of the mountain this afternoon, so they won't be entirely bored."

"Sorry about the extra shifts. Are we shorthanded?"

"Extremely, but this is the busiest week of the year so I guess extra shifts are to be expected. Next year I'll have my family visit after New Year's."

"Let me know if there's anything I can do to help."

"Actually, there is something." Dawn paused. "I just got a call from maintenance. They want the dead woman's car moved. It seems it's blocking the snowplow. They asked if I could take it over to employee parking. Do you think you could move it over there for me? I'm really swamped. It'd be a big help."

"Sure, no problem. Do you have the keys?"

Dawn handed them to her. "Just drop them back here when you're done."

"No problem. By the way, can you tell me where Carrie Brandywine and Karen Bates are working today?"

Dawn punched the names into her computer. "Carrie's on the second floor and Karen's on the fifth."

"Thanks. I'll move the car as soon as I check on their comps."

"Carrie has her boyfriend visiting. I'm not sure about Karen."

"Thanks; that'll save me some time. Hope you get some time off with your family."

"Thanks, me too."

"Let's go check with Karen; then we'll move the car," Andi suggested.

"I'm kind of surprised the resort doesn't have blackout dates on busy holidays. I'm sure you could have easily sold those rooms." Mac pushed the button for the fifth floor after everyone had boarded the elevator.

"A lot of places would, but we know it's important for our employees to be able to see their family at this time of year. It's not like they can ask for it off. Pretty much everyone is on the schedule."

The elevator arrived on the fifth floor and everyone filed out. "It looks like the cart is at the end of the hall." Andi led them to room 525. "You guys hang back. Karen's liable to say more if it's just me."

Alyson waited with the others while Andi continued forward. They couldn't see what Karen was doing, but they were able to hear the conversation.

"Karen?" Andi poked her head into the room.

"Andi, what brings you to my neck of the woods? Figured you'd be skiing. Heard they opened the lifts on the front of the mountain."

"I'm helping HR with a little paperwork. According to their records, you used employee comp nights this week. Can you tell me who they were for?"

"My brother and his wife. They're expecting their first baby. We're all so excited. I've already put in for vacation time in June so I can be there when it's born."

"Congratulations. Any word yet whether it's a boy or a girl?"

"They aren't going to find out. They said they want to be surprised. Personally, the suspense is killing me, but the birth is quite a ways off, so they might change their minds."

"Either way, I'm sure it will be a special event. Dawn said everyone's been working a lot of hours. Have you had much time to visit with your guests? I saw you go upstairs to clean up room 412 last night and now you're working here."

"It's been busy, but this is my regular shift. Last night I was called in on an emergency."

"It's too bad about what happened. I bet the cleanup wasn't at all pleasant."

"Yeah, it was a real mess. Water had completely soaked the carpet and through the floor into the room below. I'm certain they'll have to replace the carpet, maybe even the floor. It's amazing how much damage can be done by water."

"Did you have to pack up the guest's belongings?"

"Yeah, and that was kinda creepy. Going through someone's personal possessions. Luckily, she hadn't really unpacked yet, so I didn't have to pack up too much. Just a few clothes, toiletries, a novel she was reading, and a photo album."

"A photo album? Did you happen to open it at all?"

"No, I just stuck it in the box with the rest of the stuff. Didn't figure it was my place to be going through someone's private photos."

"I see your point. Well, thanks for the info. I should be going; I need to move a car for Dawn.

"Stacy had a photo album," Andi informed the others as they left the lodge and walked toward the parking lot. "If we can find out where they stored her stuff maybe we could get a look at it. It might tell us who she met last night."

"Who would know where it is?" Alyson asked.

"Dawn might. I'll ask her when I give her back the keys."

"Is this the car?" Trevor asked.

Andi checked the license number. "Looks like it."

"Check out the bumper sticker."

Chapter 8

"'Once a Marine, Always a Marine,'" Alyson read. "I'm beginning to see a pattern here. We know Mario was a marine and Bruce Long had a marine ring in his possession. Someone seems to be killing Marines."

"Or maybe specific Marines," Mac added. "My guess is that the victims are all linked based on some type of commonality. Maybe they all attended the same boot camp or served in the same unit, or they all belong to the same veterans association. There are a lot of marines in the world; they must have a more specific connection. It sounds like they were all brought here by someone. Bruce Long mentioned a reunion and Stacy King was comped by one of your employees."

"So I guess we keep looking for the link. Let's move the car, then ask Dawn if she knows where Stacy King's belongings were stored," Devon suggested.

Andi moved the car to the employee parking lot, then she and Alyson went back into the lodge to return the keys.

"All moved." Andi handed the keys back to Dawn.

"Thanks. I really appreciate it."

"By the way, do you happen to know where they've put Stacy King's belongings?"

"In one of the lockers in security, I guess. Why?"

"Just curious. Have a nice day."

"Thanks, you too."

They met the others at the Expedition, which was parked in front of the lodge. Devon had pulled into the loading zone so they wouldn't have to walk through the snow that was beginning to fall again.

"Dawn said she thought Stacy's personal belongings were stored in one of the lockers in security," Andi told the others.

"Any chance we could get a peek?" Mac asked.

"It'd be pushing it, considering we've already snuck in there twice in as many days, but we can try. We'll need a good plan, though."

"Sounds like a little brainstorming is in order," Trevor said.

"Let's finish up the comp list first," Eli suggested. "Who's left?"

"Steve and Randy, the lift operators, Charlie, and of course Bret."

"You said the lift operators would be in the pub after the lifts close. Let's see if we can find Charlie, then swing by Bret's again," Alyson said.

"Should we try the maintenance yard?" Devon asked.

"I guess. He could be anywhere, though."

"Like getting gas?" Mac asked.

"Yeah, I guess. Why?"

"Because I see a plow over in the fueling yard. Maybe it's him."

"Let's check it out," Andi said.

"Charlie. Hi, again," Andi greeted him. "Still working hard, I see."

"Tell me about it. I'm exhausted. It'd help if this snow would stop. By the time I finish plowing it's time to start again."

"I won't keep you. I'm just helping HR out. They have a record of you using comp nights this week. Can I ask who they were for?"

"My brother, although he never made it. The slide closed the road before he could get here. I'm hoping Bret will show up by the time they get the road open so I can spend some time with him."

"Why don't you just report Bret as AWOL? I'm sure HR would send someone else to help you."

"Bret's a friend of Mario's, served with him in the war. Mario was the one who got him this job, and he's always covered for him in the past when he's flaked. He told me he had a tough time and is still going through a period of adjustment. I figure Mario isn't here, so it's up to me to cover for his friend. I hope he shows up soon, though. I can't take this pace much longer."

"Have you been by his place today?" Andi asked.

"Yeah, a little while ago. There's still no sign of him. Probably hooked up with one of the female guests. It wouldn't be the first time."

"Hang in there. If you do decide to report his absence and ask for help I doubt that anyone, including Mario, would blame you."

Charlie shrugged, then paused for a moment. "Did you hear there's been another accident?"

"What happened?"

"Some guy fell off one of the lifts. Security's doing an investigation, but it looks like the safety bar on the chair wouldn't fall into place. There was an interruption in the flow when the lift somehow jammed and it stopped suddenly. Guy fell to his death."

"Oh my God. Which lift?" Andi asked.

"Patty's run, I think. It's a real shame; there seems to be so much going wrong all at once. Your poor dad must be beside himself."

"I should check on him. I'll catch you later. I hope your brother finally makes it."

"We need to get over to the mountain," Alyson said as they got into the Expedition. "There's no way I'm buying the fact that this was an accident."

"What could cause the lift to stop so abruptly?" Devon asked Andi after they were all loaded.

"The lifts are powered by generators, but even if a generator lost power the lifts would sort of glide to a stop. There must have been an obstruction of some kind to cause such an abrupt interruption."

"What are the odds that a certain skier could be targeted to ride a certain chair?" Mac asked. "If we're continuing with our theory that specific people are being targeted, a lot of variables would have to fall into place to ensure that a specific person was riding a specific chair at the exact moment the safety bar stuck and the lift met with an obstruction."

"Seems unlikely," Alyson agreed.

"Take a left at the parking lot," Andi instructed. "We'll need to park and ride the lifts up to Patty's run. It's one of our black diamond runs at the top of the hill."

"Too bad we don't have our skis; we could ski down," Eli commented.

"Somehow it doesn't look like skiing is in the cards for us. At least not today." Devon sighed.

They rode a series of lifts to the top of the mountain, where the Grizzly Mountain security patrol had Patty's run closed. The body had already been transported down the hill by the time they arrived.

"Martin, what happened?" Andi asked one of the uniformed officers.

"Lift jammed and one of the skiers fell out of his chair. Unfortunately, it happened at the worst possible spot."

"Over Crandall's Gorge?" Andi guessed.

"Exactly."

"This particular lift mostly follows the ski run and in most spots a fall from a chair probably wouldn't be fatal. But there's one spot where it crosses Crandall's Gorge and the drop increases dramatically," Andi explained to the group.

"Do you know why the safety bar failed?" Devon asked the security officer.

"Someone jammed something in the mechanism. The lift operator, Randy

Fallon, said the bar had been working fine all day. Whoever tampered with the arm must have done it during the previous run."

"Do you know what caused the lift to jam?"

"Not yet. The lift's been running fine all day. They're checking it out, but it has to have been some type of debris from the storm. Although to be honest, that seems unlikely. These lifts are built to withstand some pretty intense weather conditions."

"Do you think someone might have tampered with it?" Andi asked.

"Don't see how. Lift's been running all day. Randy said he never left his post."

Andi looked up the mountain in the direction of the lifts and frowned.

"Have there been any manual disruptions to service?" Andi asked.

"There was a brief interruption a few minutes before the accident. Randy had to manually stop the lift to load a disabled man who wanted to ride. I guess the disruption could have jarred something loose."

"Does that seem likely?" Andi asked.

"Not really, but I don't have a more likely explanation. I guess the whole thing could just have been one of those freak accidents."

"I guess. Thanks for the update." Andi and the others walked away from the crowd gathered around the loading area for the lift.

"So what do you think?" Andi asked after they'd wandered to a more isolated spot.

"This one's going to be tough to figure out. Let's head back to the house and put our heads together," Alyson suggested.

"Yeah, it's freezing out here," Mac agreed.

They rode the lifts back down to the parking lot, then drove back to the house. Alyson made coffee while Andi called her dad to see if she could find out the identity of the victim.

Alyson pulled a blanket over her lap. It seemed like she couldn't get warmed up today, no matter how hard she tried.

"Victim's name was Todd Wallford," Andi informed the others. "He was a guest at the resort. So far that's all I know. My dad wasn't answering his phone, so I called Dawn in reception."

"Maybe this one really was an accident," Trevor speculated. "You know how many variables would have to come together for this to be orchestrated for a specific victim."

"Trevor's right." Mac nodded. "But the odds of all the variables coming together at the exact time for the accident to occur are astronomical. It has to have been planned."

"Okay, let's break it down," Alyson said. "We have several separate things that had to happen for the accident to occur in the first place. The safety bar failed to close and we're assuming it was tampered with. Something jammed the operation of the lift, which, according to security, is unlikely to happen. The specific chair in question had to be exactly over an area where a fall would result in death, and if we're assuming a specific victim, that specific rider would have had to be in that specific chair at the time of the incident."

"Sounds unlikely," Andi confirmed.

"Let's start with the victim," Devon began. "For our conspiracy theory to hold true, the most recent victim should be linked with the others. Mario, Bret, Bruce, and Stacy were all marines or connected with the marines in some way. Bruce and Stacy are dead, Mario almost died, and Bret is missing. At this point we're assuming the link between all these incidences is the Marines. Is there any way we can find out more about Todd Wallford?"

"His body was taken to the clinic," Andi added. "I doubt we'll be able to get a look at it until tonight, although that might not be all that important. We already know how he died, which wasn't the case with the others."

"We need to get a look at his room," Mac announced, "hopefully before someone cleans it out."

"Let's head over to reception and I'll see what I can do." Andi rose. "It would be great if he was staying in one of the cabins; it'll be easier to break in. If he's in the lodge we'll need a diversion while I get a key."

"Back again?" Dawn asked.

"Yeah. With all the accidents I'm trying to help out where I can. Everyone seems to be on overload."

"Do you think you could watch the desk while I run to the ladies' room? I haven't had a break all day."

"Sure, no problem."

Andi slipped behind the counter as soon as Dawn ran off and quickly punched up the reservation for Todd Wallford.

"He's staying in Moose Lake Lodge, room M321. The keys for those rooms will be over there. We can head over when Dawn gets back," Andi told Alyson.

"Does the reservation form say anything else?"

"He's been here since the twenty-sixth. His home address is in San Francisco. He appears to be here alone. Hey, that's strange; he's here on an employee comp too."

"We only have three employees left," Alyson pointed out. "The two lift operators and Bret Robbins."

"I guess we'd better keep checking," Andi said.

Dawn returned. "Thanks! Things were getting a little desperate."

"No problem. Glad I could help."

Moose Lake Lodge was situated at the foot of the mountain. Skiers could ski from the front door of the lodge over to the lifts. The lodge didn't possess the same luxuries as the Grizzly Mountain Lodge, but diehard skiers preferred its proximity to the lifts. Alyson followed Andi into the rustic building.

"Hey, Andi, what are you doing in our neck of the woods?" the handsome young man behind the reception desk asked.

"I'm giving breaks. I heard we're really short-staffed today so I volunteered to help out."

"I'd love a break. Thanks tons. I'll be back in thirty."

"The room is on the third floor," Andi informed the others as soon as the desk clerk was out of sight. "Danny said he'd be back in thirty, but you'd better make it twenty just to be safe."

Alyson and the others rode the elevator to the third floor. Room 321 was decorated in the same mountain green as the rest of the resort, but it offered a spectacular view of one of the beginner runs. Skiers young and old with brightly colored jackets swished and snowplowed down the gentle slope.

They started opening drawers and closets in their search for a linking clue. As with the other rooms, the closet was filled with clothes and the bathroom with toiletries. On top of the bedside table was an empty glass and a current best seller. There was a folder with airline tickets, a car rental agreement, and various receipts in the drawer.

"I don't see anything personal," Mac said. "He must have had his wallet on him. It's probably locked up in security."

"Here's something." Eli held up a single sheet of paper.

Chapter 9

"It lists the names of the other victims." Eli handed the paper to Devon. "After each name are a few notes."

"'Mario Gonzales, explosion? Bruce Long, hypothermia? Stacy King, heart attack? Kabul?'" Devon read.

"Kabul?" Alyson asked. "What does a city in Afghanistan have to do with anything?"

"I have no idea."

"We should get back to Andi. Maybe she can get us a look at the things Todd had on him."

Alyson and the others entered the lobby just as the desk clerk was heading toward the reception area from another direction. Alyson quickly passed the key to Andi, who replaced it before the clerk approached her.

"Thanks, Andi. I'll let you get back to your friends."

"No problem. Have a good day."

"Yeah, you too."

"So what'd you find out?" Andi asked as they left the lodge and walked to the SUV.

"Not a whole lot," Alyson answered. "The victim's personal property, like his wallet, must have been on him when he died. I'm guessing it's locked up in security."

"You're not thinking about breaking into security again?"

"Actually, we were."

"Honestly, I'm running out of excuses. Someone is going to get suspicious eventually. I guess I could try the break thing again."

"It's worth a try," Alyson encouraged.

"Okay, but I go in alone this time. If I was really giving breaks I wouldn't have any friends following me around, and I'm betting whoever's on duty at security today will realize that."

"Okay, we'll wait in the Expedition," Alyson agreed.

Andi walked into the office and a few minutes later a woman in a uniform emerged.

"It looks like it worked," Mac commented. "I hope she doesn't have any problem getting into the locker."

"I still can't figure out how the murderer got the victim on that specific chair at the specific time needed," Devon said. "If he was one person ahead or one person back in the line he wouldn't have been in the correct chair even if the murderer could have figured out how to get the victim to ride that particular lift at that specific time."

"Yeah, it's a tough one." Alyson reached across the seat and took Devon's hand.

"We should head over to the bar after this," Eli suggested.

"It looks like one of the other security personnel just showed up," Mac pointed out. "I hope Andi isn't in the back."

"She's good at covering and the personnel at the resort have no reason to suspect her of doing anything wrong," Devon pointed out. "I'm sure she'll be fine."

"It looks like she's coming out," Trevor said.

Andi jogged over to the car and slipped into the back next to Trevor. She pulled a sheet of paper out of her jeans pocket.

"I found something in the man's wallet. I had no idea what it meant so I brought it with me."

"What does it say?" Mac asked.

"It's just a series of numbers: 16146138."

"It could be a code of some type," Mac guessed.

"Or maybe a phone number," Eli speculated. "It could be 1-614-6138."

"There aren't enough numbers to be an American social security number, but too many for a date. What kinds of numbers are on drivers' licenses and personal IDs in Canada?" Devon asked.

"Nothing that would match."

"Did you happen to think to check to see if Stacy King's stuff was locked up in security?" Devon asked.

"Actually, I did. Both Bruce and Stacy's bodies were evacuated by medical helicopters from Vancouver today. Their belongings were sent along with them."

"Why didn't they take Todd?" Alyson wondered.

"The accident happened after they'd left. Weather permitting, I'm sure they'll be back for him tomorrow."

"Now what?" Mac asked.

"Let's head over to the bar to see if Randy is there. We can ask him about both the accident and the comps," Alyson suggested. "Then we can go back to the house to try to make some sense of all this."

The bar was packed with thirsty skiers and employees, who had gathered to wind down after a long day on the slopes. Boisterous patrons occupied every table and every seat at the bar, with groups of people standing around nearby.

"There's Randy." Andi pointed to a long-haired man with a short beard and a silver hoop earring in one ear. "Alyson and I will go talk to him. Maybe the rest of you should hang back."

The others settled around a table by the door that had just been vacated.

"Hey, Randy. How's it going?" Andi leaned in next to him.

"Hey, Andi. Who's your friend?"

"Alyson. She's visiting from the States."

"I'm happy to meet you," Alyson said to the man, who looked like he wanted to devour her.

"Nice meeting you too. Staying long?"

"No," Alyson answered. "Not long."

The man shrugged and turned his attention back to Andi. "Did you hear about the accident we had on the lifts today? It was such a drag."

"Yeah, I heard. Any idea what happened?"

"Security tells me the chair was tampered with. I was on shift all day and didn't see anything. I'm sure the safety bar was working earlier; otherwise someone would have reported it."

"Were there any lift stoppages, manual or accidental?" Andi asked.

"Yeah, right before the accident we had a disabled man wanting to ride the lift up.

I had to stop the chairs for a minute or so while he loaded. Other than that it was a pretty quiet morning."

"Do you remember what this disabled man looked like?"

"Middle-aged. Dark hair. Seemed to get around pretty well for someone in a wheelchair. If I didn't know better I'd say the wheelchair thing was a scam, but I'm not sure why anyone would fake something like that."

"Did he ride the lift back down?" Andi wondered.

"Not as far as I saw. Guess he could have skied. Saw something on the news about disabled folks skiing."

"Did it look like he had special skis?" Alyson asked.

"No, they seemed like the normal type. Now that I think about it, the whole thing was kind of strange."

Andi looked at Alyson. She shrugged.

"Did you notice anything odd about the man who rode in the chair that had been tampered with?" Alyson asked.

Randy shrugged. "He looked like a regular skier. Seemed like a nice guy. He stopped to ask me about the resort and how I liked working here."

"Did you see anyone who was in line behind him load while he was talking to you?"

"I guess three or four others might have."

"Any idea how the lift jammed?" Alyson asked.

"None. It's been running real smooth. Of course with the storm, some debris could have gotten into the gears. Something jams one of those gears and the whole thing comes to a grinding halt. Anyway, it was a real tragedy."

"It really was," Andi agreed. "Oh, by the way, I'm helping HR out with some recordkeeping because they're so backed up. They have you on record for using comp nights this week. Do you mind telling me who they were for?"

"Some friend of Bret's. He gave me a couple hundred dollars to let him use them. I had no plans to use them any time soon so I decided to take the cash."

"Okay, thanks. Have a nice evening."

Andi and Alyson filled the others in as they drove back to the house. Due to the late hour they decided to pick up a couple of pizzas on the way for dinner.

"This pizza's really good." Trevor took a large bit of a slice from the cheesy pie.

"We have a great pizza place at home, but this is almost as good."

"Can you believe it was only last week that we were at Pirates Pizza?" Mac mused. "It seems like we've been here for months rather than days."

"A lot has happened in the past three days." Alyson picked a piece of pepperoni off the top of her slice and nibbled on the edge. "I think my brain is on overload. I'm sure there's an answer to this whole thing, but there are so many things going through my mind that I can't process anything."

"Okay, what do we know and what do we need to find out?" Trevor asked. "We went through this with the mayor's murder and it really helped us get focused."

"That's a good idea." Mac walked over to the table and picked up a tablet of paper. "Last week when we were trying to put together a series of seemingly random events at the Christmas carnival," she explained to Devon, Eli, and Andi, "we made three lists. What we knew, what we suspected but didn't have proof of, and what we didn't know but wanted to find out."

"Okay, I'm game." Devon helped himself to a second slice of pizza. "Where do we start?"

"Let's start with what we know." Mac sat poised with a pen and the pad.

"We know we have four victims," Andi started. "Mario, Bruce Long, Stacy King, and Todd Wallford."

"We know Mario was in the marines and was stationed in Afghanistan," Eli said. "We suspect Bruce and Stacy were in the marines, although a ring and a bumper sticker don't constitute proof, so I guess we should put that under things we suspect."

"We know Mario was injured in an explosion and we suspect it was deliberate," Andi added. "We also suspect Charlie got food poisoning and we suspect that was deliberate."

"We know both Stacy and Todd were staying here on employee comps," Trevor said. "We know Bret bought Randy's for Todd and we suspect he used his own for Stacy."

"We also know Bret served in the military with Mario," Mac said as she wrote. "I'm seeing Bret as the common link. Question is, is he the murderer or is he another victim? I guess that should go on the things-we-want-to-know page."

"We suspect both Bruce and Stacy were poisoned," Alyson said. "We still need to check that out. Maybe we should add a to-do page."

"Good idea." Mac turned the page and added *do drug test* to that side.

"We suspect Todd was murdered—that his fall wasn't an accident—but we have no idea how the killer pulled it off," Trevor joined in. "I guess we should put *figure out how Todd was killed* on the to-do page."

"We also have a note that appears to be in code," Andi reminded them. "Should we add *break code* to the to-do page?"

"We need to get a look at Bret's condo," Devon pointed out. "Add that to our to-do page."

"So far we have *drug test the alcohol, check out Bret's condo, break the code*, and *figure out how Todd was killed* on the to-do list," Mac read. "Where do we start?"

"This is a good time to go to the lab because it should be closed," Andi told them. "It isn't a good time to break into Bret's apartment because most of the employees are off shift now. We could stop by there, though, to see if he's there. If we need to break in we'll have to do it tomorrow when everyone's working."

"Sounds like a plan. Just let me wash up." Alyson stood up and went upstairs.

As before, the clinic was dark. Andi let them in and they headed straight to the lab. After an extensive search they finally found the drug test kits they were looking for.

Mac set up a work station on one of the counters and set to work testing the scotch from Bruce Long's bottle and his blood sample.

"We have a match," she said after several minutes. "The scotch tests positive for GHB. The blood sample from Bruce also tests positive for GHB."

"So we have our proof. Maybe we should tell someone at this point," Alyson suggested.

"Let's do it in the morning," Andi countered. "It'll give us a chance to work on the other clues and check out Bret's condo. Besides, I might be grounded for life once we tell my dad what we've been doing and I'd like one more night with all of you."

"Okay, you'll talk to him tomorrow," Mac agreed. "Let's go back to the house to see if we can figure out the code."

"And the *how* to Todd's murder," Alyson reminded them. "I don't suppose there's any way we could get a look at security's report on his death? There might be a clue."

"I'll give it a try," Andi volunteered. "Let's head over to the office and I'll see what I can do."

Andi walked into the office and back out with a folder five minutes later.

"You got it?" Mac asked.

She nodded. "I just told security that my dad sent me over to get a copy of the report. He didn't even blink an eye. I figure unless my dad asks for a copy on his own, we're probably in the clear."

"Way to go, Andi." Trevor kissed her hard on the lips.

The gang returned to the house and settled in. In spite of their best efforts the meaning of the numbers seemed elusive.

"I've been looking at these numbers until I'm cross-eyed and I don't see any recognizable pattern." Mac leaned against the sofa from her spot on the floor. "If you apply a substitution cipher, the corresponding letters are either AFADFACH or PNFMH, or maybe AFNFMH. Any way you slice it, it doesn't look like a word."

"Maybe it's a substitution cipher with a specific key," Devon suggested.

"If it is we'll never solve it without the key. It could still be a phone number, or maybe some type of ID number."

"Maybe the numbers don't have anything to do with what we're working on," Trevor mused. "It was in the victim's wallet; it might just be a pin number or a password he wanted to remember."

"True," Mac acknowledged. "Maybe we're seeing a clue where there isn't one. Let's move on to the *how* part of our brainstorming session."

"Maybe we should pick this up in the morning." Alyson yawned. "My brain is too tired to storm."

"Yeah, I should get home too." Andi stood up. "I'll bring pastries again. Maybe we'll be able to figure it out in the morning, when we have fresh brains."

Chapter 10

Andi showed up bright and early the next morning. She'd brought pastries from the bakery and a variety of sliced fruit and cooked breakfast meat from the resort buffet.

"Looks good." Trevor helped himself to a large plateful.

"It's snowing again." Mac groaned.

"The partial clearing we were promised never really materialized. Our next shot for clear skies is tomorrow, Are you okay?" Andi asked Alyson. "You look sort of pale."

"I'm okay. Just tired."

"You should eat some of these oranges. If you're getting a cold the vitamin C will do you good. Cookie imports them from Florida. They're really good."

"Thanks." Alyson picked up a small slice.

"What time do you think it will be safe to head over to Bret's?" Devon asked.

"Maybe around ten. Even the folks who only work a half day should be gone by then."

Mac looked at the clock over the stove. "It's nine o'clock now. Let's eat, then check out the condo. We can work on the security file this afternoon."

"Maybe Bret's there and we won't have to break in." Trevor poured himself some coffee.

"That would be preferable," Andi agreed. "At some point I'm going to have to explain to my dad everything we've done, and the less criminal activity I have to confess the better."

A knock on Bret's door confirmed that there still wasn't an answer. Luckily, the surrounding condos all appeared to be deserted. Devon found a rock and broke the small window near the door. He reached his hand inside and turned the lock.

"This place is a mess," Eli observed. "I don't see any dead bodies, though."

"If there are any clues we'll never find them." Alyson stepped over a large pile of dirty laundry.

"There's food on the dishes in the kitchen that looks like it's been there since the turn of the century," Mac informed them.

"How can anyone live this way?" Andi wondered. "I doubt we'll find anything useful."

"And then again, maybe we will. Look at this." Trevor stood in front of the closet door. The entire closet was full of explosives. Different types, different levels of power.

"Oh my God. Do you think he's the one who blew up the propane tank?" Andi asked.

"Maybe. He obviously had the fire power to do it."

"But why? Bret and Mario were friends."

"Maybe it's a coincidence," Alyson suggested. "Just because he has explosives doesn't mean he tried to kill Mario."

"What could he possibly want with all this stuff?" Mac wondered. "There's enough fire power for him to start his own war."

"I'd better call my dad," Andi said. "I'm not sure how I'm going to explain how we happened to be in Bret's condo, but I think it's time to fill him in."

Andi called her father and Devon called his.

"Andi," her dad called as he entered the condo, with Devon's father on his heels a short while later.

"Here, Dad," Andi answered from the back of the bedroom.

"You said Bret had a bunch of explosives?"

"Here in the closet."

Andi's dad walked over to the closet and pulled out his two-way radio. "Sebastian."

"Yeah, boss?" Alyson heard a voice on the other end reply.

"Send a security team over to Bret Robbins's condo. Right away."

"Sure thing."

After he put his radio away he turned to look at Andi. "Okay, you want to tell me how you happened to find this stuff?"

"It's kind of a long story. And there's more. Possibly a lot more," Andi said softly. "This place is a dump. Do you think we should go somewhere else to talk?"

"You kids head over to the conference room. As soon as security gets here to dispose of these explosives I'll meet you there," Andi's dad instructed.

"I am so dead." Andi groaned as they drove toward the admin offices.

"We didn't actually do anything wrong," Trevor insisted. "Okay, maybe a little breaking and entering, but it was for a good cause."

"Let's get the scotch and the positive test strips," Andi suggested. "Maybe we can leave out the test on the blood. We have enough without it, and that might really make my dad flip."

Once they'd gathered everything they needed, they headed over to the admin offices to wait for the dads. Alyson could tell Andi was really sweating her dad's reaction when he arrived, but it had taken only a moment to tell the man adored his daughter and would do anything to make sure she was safe and happy. It was times like this that Alyson missed her own father. The fact that she'd most likely never see him again didn't even seem real most of the time.

"Would someone like to tell me what's going on?" Andi's dad asked as soon as he arrived and had asked everyone to take a seat around the conference table.

"The night Bruce Long's body was found," Devon began, "we happened to meet Andi in the cantina. We asked her to join us for dinner, and during the course of the meal she told us about Mario's accident. We thought it a little odd that there could be two such serious accidents in a two-day period, so we began to wonder if they weren't accidents at all."

"You thought someone purposely hurt Mario and killed Bruce Long?" Devon's dad asked.

"At this point, yes," Devon answered. "But it took a little sleuthing on our part to put together all the pieces."

"Oh, this should be good." Devon's dad sighed. "My sons and their friends consider themselves to be amateur detectives of some sort. They're actually very good, so I have a feeling we're in for a hell of a story."

"So you decided the accidents might not be accidents..." Andi's dad said encouragingly.

"We thought it might be helpful if we could get a look at Bruce Long's body," Mac contributed.

"You broke into the clinic!"

"Actually, I have a key," Andi reminded him.

"Anyway," Mac continued, "a cursory examination of the victim revealed a bump on the back of his head and skin under his fingernails." She passed the skin sample to Andi's dad.

"We realized the bump could have happened when he passed out and the skin could have come from anywhere," Alyson said, "but we felt further investigation was warranted."

"Do I even want to hear this?" Andi's dad asked.

"Probably not," Andi answered, "but it's important. Just remember I love you and we were only trying to help."

"The next day," Devon continued, "we decided to check out Bruce Long's cabin. We didn't find much there except a note by the phone that said 'pub eight p.m.' Mr. Long's body was found around nine o'clock, so the period of time between the meeting at the pub and finding the body was suspiciously short."

"We talked to Hank," Andi added. "He said Mr. Long ordered a forty-year-old bottle of scotch he didn't even know he had. Mr. Long had mentioned a reunion, but no one ever showed up to join him. Hank said he had one drink and left."

"One drink doesn't sound like enough to make someone pass out in the snow," Andi's dad commented.

"That's what we thought." Alyson jumped in. "I bought the bottle from Hank. We used drug test kits we found in the clinic to test it. It came up positive for GHB. A strong enough dose of GHB would cause someone to feel dizzy almost immediately and to pass out within a matter of minutes."

"You think someone drugged Bruce Long?" Andi's dad clarified.

"We do. At the time we had little to go on, but now we have quite a lot of evidence," Alyson explained.

"Besides investigating Mr. Long's death," Mac continued the story, "we also looked into Mario's accident. We talked to Charlie in maintenance and learned that he was actually on shift the day of Mario's accident but somehow got food poisoning, so Mario was called in to cover for him."

"You think someone specifically targeted Mario?" Devon's dad asked.

"We do." Mac nodded. "We found out along the way that both Mario and Bruce Long were marines. We also suspect the woman who had the heart attack, Stacy King, was a marine. Although we don't have definitive proof, she had a bumper sticker on her car that said 'Once a Marine, Always a Marine.'"

"So you think someone's targeting marines," Andi's dad concluded.

"Specific marines," Devon said. "During a conversation with Charlie, we learned that Bret was in the same marine unit as Mario in Afghanistan. He's been AWOL for two days; Charlie's been covering for him. We broke into his condo because we thought he might be another victim. Now we're not so sure."

"To summarize, you think Bruce Long and Stacy King were both killed by the same person, who also tried to kill Mario, and that their deaths have something to do with the fact that they were all marines," Andi's dad clarified.

"Yes," Alyson answered.

"And you think Bret is either the killer or another victim?" he added.

"Yes," Alyson said again.

"As crazy as this sounds, I think you've made a good case for yourselves. It might be better if you didn't fill me in on all the details of how you got this information. I'd hate to have to have my own daughter arrested."

"There's more." Andi hesitated. "We think the accident on the lifts yesterday was deliberate sabotage. We haven't figured out how yet, but we did confirm that the victim, Todd Wallford, was here as Bret's guest. We think Stacy King was here as his guest also. I found out that Bret used some of his points this week and Randy Fallon told me Bret bought some of his comp nights from him."

"I'm not sure whether to be grateful or horrified by what you kids have been up to." Andi's dad shook his head. "But from this point on I want you to let our security people handle the situation. Go home, relax, have a nice dinner, take a sleigh ride, go skiing tomorrow. The weather report is calling for sunshine. Have fun, but promise me you'll leave this alone. If someone *is* orchestrating all these deaths you guys might be putting yourselves in trouble by snooping around."

"I promise." Andi hugged her dad.

Chapter 11

After leaving the conference room they headed over to the house. Alyson made a pot of hot cider and Mac heated up crab puffs and salmon rolls in the oven. Devon built a fire and Eli put on some music. There was a gentle snow falling outside the large picture windows, creating a feeling of romantic isolation.

"So where should we have dinner tonight?" Trevor asked as Alyson carried in a tray of hot beverages.

"Let's go to the lodge," Andi suggested. "Maybe we can relax and enjoy it this time. I'll call Tony about a reservation."

"Sounds good." Trevor put his arm around Andi's shoulders.

"I want to stop off in the village and buy a bathing suit." Alyson sat down next to Devon. "I've been wanting to try out that hot tub ever since we've been here."

"There's a great little shop across from the pub," Andi told her. "I'm due for a new suit myself. Plus I can get us all an employee discount."

"Count me in." Mac set down the tray of appetizers on the coffee table. "My budget's kind of limited, but I'm sure I can find something."

"This is really nice." Alyson placed her head on Devon's shoulder. "This is the first time I've felt relaxed since we've been here."

"It has been a bit of a ride," Trevor admitted.

"When I was at home in Cutter's Cove I envisioned sleigh rides, gourmet dinners, romantic moments beside a roaring fire, and world-class skiing. Not death and conspiracy," Alyson complained.

"I can order us a sleigh to take us into town," Devon offered.

"Really? I'd like that. Will it fit all six of us?"

"It should."

"I'll need to go home and change at some point," Andi reminded them.

"Trevor can take you home later. We'll pick you up first, then head over to the bikini shop and then to dinner," Devon suggested.

"I can't believe my dad didn't totally flip out." Andi curled up into Trevor's side. "I really expected him to go ballistic and lock me in my room for life, if not longer."

"Maybe he realized we were doing the work his security personnel should have been doing," Eli pointed out. "And with us there it was kind of hard for him to lose his cool. I'm sure he wanted to maintain a professional air."

"I can't believe you guys do this all the time. Tell me about some of your other investigations," Andi said.

"We first met when Alyson moved to Cutter's Cove last September," Trevor began.

"You've only known each other since September? You seem so close. I would have guessed you were lifelong friends."

"We only met three days ago," Trevor pointed out. "And I feel pretty close to you. Solving a mystery breeds intimacy pretty quickly."

"I guess you're right. Continue with your story."

"Alyson and her mom bought this old mansion on a bluff overlooking the Pacific Ocean. The attic was jam-packed with generations of both valuable artwork and antiques and quite a lot of garbage. Mac and I, along with Eli, volunteered to help her clean it out. Somewhere along the way we got the idea of seeing if we could find the rightful heir to the stuff."

"And did you? Find the heir?"

"We did. Of course along the way Alyson almost got shot and we uncovered a double murder and a history of extortion."

"You're kidding?"

"Not a bit. But everything turned out okay and we've been best friends ever since."

"I wish I lived near you guys. It sounds like you have a lot of fun. Things here are nice, and I have several close friends, but I've never solved a murder."

"In the four months we've known one another we've solved four murders, three kidnappings, and two secret conspiracies."

"And let's not forget the fact that Alyson broke a hundred-year-old curse," Mac reminded him.

"Oh, you have to tell me about that."

For the next several hours they filled Andi in on their various adventures until it was time for her to go home and change for dinner.

Alyson put on soft suede pants and a warm cashmere sweater for dinner. She curled the ends of her long hair and applied a light touch of makeup.

Mac wore one of Alyson's long wool skirts with thick leggings underneath to keep her warm. She wore a fuzzy angora sweater and, like Alyson, had curled her long hair in a soft, flowing style.

"You both look wow," Trevor complimented them when they came downstairs. "We should do this dress-up thing more often."

"You look nice yourself. New sweater?" Mac asked.

"My mom gave it to me for Christmas. What do you think?"

"I like it." Alyson looped her arm through Trevor's and walked into the living room, where Devon and Eli were waiting.

"Sleigh's here." Devon got up from the sofa and walked over to take Alyson from Trevor's arm. "You look beautiful."

"Why, thank you, kind sir."

Devon helped Alyson into her coat while Eli helped Mac into hers. The sleigh had three rows of passenger seats. Devon and Alyson climbed into the back row, Eli and Mac into the middle, and Trevor into the front.

The snow from earlier in the day had stopped and the clouds had cleared to reveal a sky decorated with more stars than any of them had ever seen. Each seat of the sleigh held a heavy blanket, which each of the couples and Trevor snuggled under.

"Mind holding off with the smoochies until we pick up Andi?" Trevor complained. "I feel a little left out."

"Don't look." Alyson laughed as she wrapped her arms around Devon's neck for a prolonged kiss.

"I can hear you."

"So don't listen," Mac added as she scootched down under the blanket for a little one-on-one time with Eli.

"Can this thing go any faster?" Trevor asked the driver.

"Don't worry, we're almost at Andi's. I've known her since she was born, though, so watch the hands."

"Great. We have our very own watchdog along. Did Andi's dad arrange for you to be our driver?"

"No, it's my shift. I guess you just lucked out. The other driver is new. I'm not sure he's even met Andi yet."

Andi had been waiting for them and jogged out of the house as soon as the sleigh pulled up. Trevor hopped down to help her into the high seat.

"Where to?" the driver asked.

"Can we just drive around a bit?" Andi asked. "We have dinner reservations at eight and we wanted to stop by the bathing suit shop beforehand, but we should have time for a backwoods tour."

"Whatever you want, darlin'. I already warned your young man about being a gentleman at all times."

"Rory, you didn't. I'm not ten anymore. I'm perfectly capable of monitoring my own dating activity. I don't need a watchdog along."

"That's what I said," Trevor agreed. "Besides, I'm always a gentleman." He pulled the blanket over Andi and himself so that the watchful driver could only imagine what was going on.

The sleigh traveled a narrow path through the forest. The thick canopy of evergreen branches blocked the light from the sky in places, causing a feeling of total isolation from the rest of the world. Each of the couples was locked in their own intimate exchange of quietly spoken words and long, meaningful kisses. By the time the sleigh returned to the village and the bathing suit shop, all involved welcomed the shot of cold air to cool their senses.

"I think I'll get this red one." In the shop, Alyson held up a teeny-tiny bikini made of red satin.

"I think I'll stick with a one piece," a more modest Mac said. "I saw a nice one in royal blue when we first walked in."

"Come on, Mac. Take a walk on the wild side," Alyson encouraged. "How about this one?" She held up a modestly cut two-piece in forest green. "The green will look great with your complexion."

"I don't know…"

"Just try it on." Alyson pushed her into a nearby dressing room. "What are you getting?" she asked Andi.'

"Maybe this black one." She held up a black bikini with silver trim in a Brazilian style.

"It's cute. Don't you think it's cute, Trevor?"

"Cute isn't the word I was going for. But yeah, I like it."

"How's it going?" Alyson called out to Mac.

"I don't know. I'm not sure it's me."

"Can I see?"

"Is Eli there? Or any of the guys, for that matter?"

"I'll come in alone."

"Okay. But don't laugh."

The bathing suit showed off Mac's figure and complexion perfectly.

"Wow, you're a total babe. You have to get it. Eli will totally lose his cookies when he sees you."

"Are you sure? I feel sort of naked."

"Wait here."

Alyson walked over to the cover-ups and found a complementary color. The fabric was sheer but slightly darker than the two-piece. Alyson went back into the dressing room and slipped it over Mac's head.

"Just wear this until you're ready to get into the hot tub, then slip it off and slide in. It'll be dark. No one will get more than a brief glimpse of the hot package underneath."

"I do feel better. Less exposed. I guess it'll be okay. But remember, no porch lights."

"I promise. We'll have nothing but the stars to light our way. It may feel strange now, but you'll thank me later."

As before, Andi had reserved a table in a corner alcove with windows on three sides. This time the sky was clear and the view was breathtaking. Someone was playing a piano in the bar, and the sounds of soft jazz filled the restaurant. Candles flickered from every table, and the low lighting lent a romantic quality to the evening.

"Good evening, Miss Andi and guests," the waiter greeted them. "Can I get you beverages while you look over the menu?"

"What do you have that's sinful?" Andi asked.

"We have a nice virgin daiquiri," the waiter suggested. "I'm afraid that's as sinful as you can get when you're only sixteen."

"It's such a drag to go to a restaurant where everyone knows you," Andi complained. "I could totally pass for eighteen, which is the legal drinking age here, in any other restaurant."

"A virgin daiquiri sounds great," Mac agreed.

"Daiquiris all around?" Trevor asked.

Alyson studied the menu. "Everything looks so good."

"We have to have the crab wontons and oriental shrimp appetizers," Andi told them. "They're both to die for. Take my word for it, you won't be disappointed."

"Sounds good. When the waiter comes back with our drinks we'll have him get them started," Devon said.

"What's in the house salad?" Alyson asked.

"It's really good. It has your usual veggies, lettuce, tomato, cucumber, carrots. But it also has artichoke hearts, bay shrimp flown in fresh, feta cheese crumbles, and the best homemade dressing you've ever tasted. Of course Cookie's soup of the day is always excellent too, so it's usually a tough choice between the two. They're both pretty big servings, though, so you should probably do one or the other or you'll never be able to eat an entree."

"Any idea what the soup of the day is?" Eli asked.

"It usually says on the back of the menu." Andi turned her menu over. "Cream of roasted chestnut amaretto. Sounds decadent."

"One of us should get the salad and one of us the soup, then we'll share," Alyson suggested to Devon.

"Sounds like a plan."

"Do you want to do that too?" Mac asked Eli.

"If you do."

"Let's all do it. You really should try both," Andi said.

When the waiter returned they ordered the appetizers and toasted the evening with their fancy drinks. The bartender had added fruit garnishments, making the drinks appear tropical and exotic.

"So what's everyone eating?" Alyson asked. "I'm leaning toward the lobster."

"I think I'll try the prime rib," Devon said.

"I was leaning toward the sirloin," Mac joined in. "It says it has a blue cheese and crab topping. And it comes with asparagus. I love asparagus."

"I think I'll have the same." Eli set his menu aside.

"I'm with Alyson," Andi said. "The lobster is always excellent."

"Trevor?" Alyson asked

"I'm thinking the surf and turf. Might as well have a little variety."

The food, as usual, was excellent. They kept the conversation light, getting to know one another even better. Andi told them about growing up at the resort and attending boarding school in Vancouver, and the others filled her in on life in Cutter's Cove and their state-champion football team. By the end of the meal, it was obvious they'd be lifelong friends with Andi.

The sleigh ride back to the house was more direct than the one into the village but equally romantic. By the time they arrived, everyone was relaxed and mellow. Cold drinks in the hot tub, surrounded by snow and majestic mountains, were just the thing to top off the perfect evening.

Alyson hurried out of the house in front of Mac. "Mac's a little insecure about her new bathing suit, so no one say a word. Actually, Eli can say something, but privately. Trevor, no sly comments or catcalls."

"Would I do that?" Trevor asked innocently.

"You would, but don't."

"My lips are sealed."

Alyson gave him a hard stare.

"I promise."

Mac shyly walked out of the house and hesitated.

"We totally forgot about looking through the security report on Todd Wallford's death," Alyson said, trying to divert everyone's attention away from Mac.

"We'll do it tomorrow." Devon nuzzled Alyson's neck.

Alyson saw Mac slip off her cover-up and slide into the tub. Eli whispered something to her and she turned beet red, but she was smiling.

"Do you know if the forecast is still for a clear sky?" Alyson asked.

"As far as I know. It should be a great day for skiing. You guys in? I know all the best runs," Andi offered.

"Sounds good," Alyson answered. "I was beginning to think I'd end up going home without trying out the world-class slopes I've been hearing about."

"Have you skied a lot?" Andi asked.

"Yeah, mostly in Europe and on the East Coast. East Coast slopes can't really compare to European ones."

"I thought you were from Minnesota." Trevor shook his head. "You haven't skied

Colorado? They have some awesome runs."

"Yeah, of course I have. My parents just liked to vacation on the East Coast," Alyson explained. "Vermont, mostly."

"I noticed a tram going up the hill earlier." Mac changed the subject. "Some of the people didn't even have skis. Is there something else up there besides ski runs?"

"Yeah, sort of a miniresort. There's a restaurant, a pool that's enclosed in the winter and open in the summer, an ice-skating rink, and a really fantastic spa. There's also an arcade and a workout center."

"An alternative with a view," Mac summarized

"Exactly. Of course it's only open when the wind allows the tram to operate, so it's not really an alternative on the days the lifts are closed. It's really nice, though. We should go up for lunch tomorrow. On a clear day the views are spectacular."

"This is so relaxing." Alyson leaned her head against the back of the tub as revolving jets circulated the water. "I can't believe how clear it is. The sky looks so big here. And the stars; I had no idea there were so many stars."

"The air is thin at this altitude, plus it's very dark here. Very few streetlights. The nights can be really spectacular. Oh, look, a shooting star." Andi pointed into the night sky.

"I bet it's spectacular sitting out here when there's a meteor shower," Mac speculated.

"Yeah, it's really something. Summers are the best for sky watching unless you have a hot tub, though. It can get pretty cold at night in the winter."

"It seems cold tonight. Even colder than it was during the blizzard, if that's possible," Trevor commented.

"The temperature always drops after a storm. Be sure to dress warm tomorrow. Lots of layers. I doubt the temperature will even get close to zero."

"Oh, look, another shooting star." Mac pointed into the sky. "That one looked close. If I didn't know better I'd bet it hit earth somewhere."

"Some fragments of a meteor did hit earth not too long ago," Devon told them. "It must have been something, seeing those streak through the sky."

"What's that over there?" Eli asked. "That bright glow off to the left? You don't think that streak of light really hit earth, do you?"

"I doubt it, but I see what you're talking about." Mac sat forward and tried to make out what they were looking at. "What's over there?"

Andi tried to get her bearings. "Nothing much. A few of the more isolated cabins."

"Well, I think one of them is on fire." Mac stood up.

"I'd better call it in." Andi got out of the tub and grabbed a towel.

"So much for our romantic evening," Trevor grumbled.

"Come on, we'd better get dressed." Mac got out of the tub and followed Andi inside.

A few minutes later a siren rang out, notifying the volunteer firefighters that their services were needed. More sirens could be heard in the distance. They were dressed and on the road within ten minutes.

"Oh, God. It is one of the cabins." Andi groaned. "I hope no one was inside. It looks like a total loss."

Flames shot high into the air, threatening to catch the limbs of the trees surrounding the cabin. Volunteer firefighters were working frantically in an attempt to keep the flames from spreading. Andi's dad pulled up and the gang ran over to his vehicle.

"Do you know if anyone was inside?" Andi asked.

"Not at this point. By the time the fire department arrived the cabin was totally engulfed. It shouldn't have gone up that fast. It's likely some type of accelerant was used."

"You think someone did this on purpose?"

"I'm betting that's what the investigation will show."

"We need to find out who was staying in this cabin. With the other events that have occurred in the past week this looks like another murder."

Andi's dad reached into his car for his two-way radio. "Get me registration," he instructed whoever was on the other end of the line.

"Yes, sir." Alyson heard a female voice answer a few seconds later.

"Can you tell me who was staying in cabin 92?'

A few seconds passed. Then they heard, "Martha Strom. She just arrived today. She'd arranged for a private helicopter to bring her in."

"What do we know about her?" Andi's dad asked.

"She arrived alone. Mentioned she was here to meet an old friend. Seemed pretty excited about it. Her registration information lists her home address as Pittsburgh, Pennsylvania."

"Has she made any in-house charges since she's been here? Maybe for dinner?"

"Her account shows she had an early meal in the lodge. The charge came through at six thirty."

"Okay, thanks."

"I'm betting she was already back in her cabin and sound asleep when the fire started," Andi speculated. "And I also think that if we dig deeper, we'll find that she was a marine."

"I hope you're wrong, but I suspect you're right." He shook his head. "I'm going to go have a talk with security; you kids stay out of the way."

Andi's dad walked over to where the security patrol had gathered.

"Let's head over to the lodge and see what we can find out about the meal that was charged to the room," Devon said.

"My dad wants us to stay out of this," Andi reminded him.

"We won't be putting ourselves in any danger or breaking into any locked buildings. We're just going to ask a question," Mac said to justify their plan.

"Okay, let's go."

Tony confirmed that Martha had shown up alone but told her waiter she was meeting someone. She'd waited for over a half hour before she received an in-house call, after which she'd ordered and dined on her own. Someone had had a bottle of wine delivered to her table, though Tony wasn't sure where it had come from.

After speaking to Tony, they decided to check the phone records the next day and headed back to the fire, which continued to burn hotly, barely reacting at all to the gallons of water the firemen sprayed on it. They all huddled together until the flames were finally extinguished. It was several hours later until the debris cooled enough for the firefighters to confirm that there was indeed a body inside, burned beyond recognition.

Chapter 12

The next morning Alyson dragged herself downstairs, still dressed in pajamas and fuzzy slippers. She pulled a large sweatshirt over her pajama top and curled up into the corner of the sofa.

"You'd better get dressed," Mac instructed her. "Andi will be here any minute. She's bringing pastries from the bakery again."

"Not hungry."

"Okay, what about skiing?"

"I'm not feeling all that well. I think I'm coming down with something." Alyson sneezed. "You guys go ahead."

"You've looked a little pale the past couple of days." Mac placed a hand on her friend's forehead. "No fever, though."

"I'll be fine. You guys go have fun."

"I don't know. I hate to leave you here alone."

"I'll stay," Devon volunteered. "I've already gotten in two weeks of skiing. It looks like we got the Internet connection back and I have a little computer work to catch up on. I also want to check out the phone records from last night's calls."

"Are you sure?" Mac asked. "'Cause I can stay."

"I'm sure."

"I'll make you some tea before I go," Mac offered.

"With lemon and honey," Alyson called after her.

Andi arrived a few minutes later and the others enjoyed their pastries and coffee while Alyson nursed her tea. Devon plugged his laptop into the wall near the couch where Alyson was sitting and began checking e-mails.

"Is the rest of the world still there?" Alyson asked. "I've felt so isolated since we've been here. No television, no phones, no Internet."

"Yeah, it looks like the earth managed to continue to revolve without our help. The Lakers won again."

"You really like those Los Angeles teams. I remember you were supporting the Dodgers in your baseball debate the other day."

"I grew up in LA. It feels like home."

"Have you ever thought about going back? Now that you're eighteen and basically graduated from high school."

"Actually ..."

"I guess we're ready," Mac interrupted. "I can come back in a few hours to check on you."

"Go. Have fun. I'll be fine."

"Okay, if you're sure…"

"Very sure.

"Hope you feel better. We'll be back this afternoon."

"Okay, 'bye," Alyson called after her.

"Can I get you anything?" Devon asked.

"Maybe a blanket."

"I'll be right back."

Devon found a blanket upstairs and wrapped it around Alyson. He kissed her on the forehead and added another log to the fire.

"You didn't have to stay, you know. I can take care of myself."

"I know. I really wanted to get some work done anyway."

"Maybe now that the Internet is up we can find a connection between the victims."

"I thought we promised to leave it alone."

"Andi promised to leave it alone. I didn't promise anything. Did you?"

"No, I guess not. Okay, let's make a list of what we know and I'll see what I can find."

"Let's start with Mario Gonzales," Alyson suggested. "He's worked here for about five years. Before that he was in Afghanistan. He went to medical school on a military grant but never worked as a doctor after returning from the war. According to his sister, something happened that changed his life."

"Do we know where he went to school or where he lived before his stint in Afghanistan?" Devon asked.

"I don't remember anyone saying. Although it might be in his personnel file."

"Okay, who else?"

"Bruce Long. A guest who was drugged, then froze to death. I'm trying to remember where he was from."

"I seem to remember Calgary."

"Yeah, I think you're right." Alyson sneezed.

"God bless you. Do we know anything else other than that he was a marine? Or at least he had a marine ring. It could have been his dad's or something."

"True. I guess we'll have to operate on the marine assumption for now."

"Okay, then we have Stacy King. She suffered a heart attack, we suspect after being drugged. Also assumed to be a marine. Although, again, a bumper sticker doesn't necessarily prove anything."

"I guess our theory is predicated on quite a few assumptions," Alyson acknowledged.

"Then there's Todd Wallford. We have no idea whether he was a marine."

"Yeah. I should go through the security report."

"Do we know anything at all about last night's victim?" Devon asked.

"Other than the fact that her name was Martha Strom and that she checked in yesterday and was meeting an old friend, not really. Except for the fact that she was supposedly stood up for dinner and someone had a bottle of wine delivered to her."

"And then there's Bret Robbins. Our could-be victim, could-be murderer, could-be-tucked-away-with-a-hot-babe dark horse."

"At least we have confirmation that he was in the marines and served with Mario," Alyson pointed out.

"He also has a fondness for explosives."

"Okay, so what now?"

"Let me surf around a bit to see what I can find. Do you need some more tea?"

"Yeah, but I'll get it. You work."

"Yes, ma'am."

"Devon," Alyson called from the kitchen.

"Yeah?"

"Do you think the others are in any danger? I mean, if whoever is doing this has been paying any attention at all they must know we've been snooping around."

"Chances are whoever is doing this is focused on specific victims, but it wouldn't hurt for all of us to be careful. The gang will be in very public places all day. They should be fine."

"I hope so." Alyson returned to the room and curled up in her spot on the sofa. She rearranged the blanket over her legs and took a sip of her tea. She opened the security folder and started to read.

"I found something on Stacy King," Devon informed her. "She graduated from Princeton at the top of her class. She majored in international studies. She did four years in Afghanistan before taking a job with the United Nations."

"Wow, impressive. At least we've confirmed she was actually a marine and didn't just have the bumper sticker."

The house phone rang.

"I'll get it," Devon offered.

"Hello. Oh, hi, Dad. They did? Really? Okay, thanks. 'Bye."

"What was that all about?"

"They've completed their investigation of the fire. It was started with a wireless detonator. Pretty high-tech. Whoever planted it knew what they were doing. The cabin had been doused with an accelerant, so the minute the bomb went off the whole place was enflamed. There's no way anyone inside could have gotten out."

"Wow, poor Martha. It was Martha, wasn't it?"

"They think so. They can't make a positive ID at this point, but Martha Strom hasn't turned up at the registration desk wondering what happened to her cabin."

"And the detonator...Did they compare it to the stuff in Bret's closet?"

Devon nodded. "It looks like it matches the other stuff he had. They're assuming at this point that he's the killer, although there's a fringe theory that someone killed him and is using his stuff."

"Anything else?"

"Dad just wants us to be careful. It looks like the killer is still out there. Who knows if and when he or she will stop?"

"Dev, can you pass me that box of tissues?"

"Still feeling funky?"

"Yeah, but I'll be okay."

"You should eat something. How about some soup?"

"Maybe in a little while. Right now I just want to sip my tea and try to solve a murder."

"Any idea how old Mario was?" Devon asked. "Mario Gonzales is a common name. We need something to narrow it down."

"Well, he went through medical school, then did a stint in the military. He's worked here for five years. Assuming he started college right out of high school and took a normal amount of time to finish, I'd say he's in his midthirties."

"Maybe I should try looking up military records."

"Can you do that?" Alyson asked.

"The amount of information I can access on my laptop is limited, but there are things that are public record. It's too bad I don't have my home computer. I could get most anything on there, given enough time."

"I wonder if the guys are having fun. It's such a nice day. I bet the skiing is over the top."

"Yeah, I bet it is. Get some rest and maybe you'll feel like going tomorrow. Can you believe tomorrow is already the thirty-first? New Year's is in two more days. It seems like this year has flown by."

"I'm looking forward to the New Year's Eve party. Andi made it sound so elegant. I haven't done elegant for a long time. Maybe I'll go into the village to see if I can find a new dress."

"I thought you were sick."

"I am, but it doesn't take much energy to shop. Besides, I want to look nice for you."

"You always look nice. Right now, pigtails, overlarge sweatshirt, fuzzy slippers, still hotter than anyone else."

"You're just saying that so I don't sneeze on you and give you my cold."

"No, seriously, hotter than anyone."

"You're sweet. A liar, but sweet. I hope I'm feeling better for the party. I want to dance all night and forget about murder and mayhem for once this holiday season. Between the 'Grizzly Mountain Killer' and the mayor's murder last week—was it really only last week? Anyway, I'd like one perfect holiday moment."

"We're alone now. I can think of something pretty perfect."

"You type, I'll shut up," Alyson said. "I can see I've got you all distracted."

"Ah, here we are: Mario Gonzales. It looks like although Mario was a medic in the war he served with a field unit rather than in a hospital."

"Field unit?"

"Yeah, the guys who actually go into the villages and shoot down bad guys."

"What a drag. He spends years learning how to save lives and they send him over there to take them. It makes no sense."

"I guess the guys in the trenches need someone with medical training too. It makes sense that they'd want someone who could respond immediately."

"Poor Mario," Alyson sympathized. "No wonder he wanted to hide away. I can't imagine dealing with something like that. It must be like living a nightmare every second of the day."

"Yeah; from what I've heard things were pretty awful over there."

"Charlie said Bret served with Mario. Have you found anything on him? Anything that might explain why he might want to kill a bunch of people over the Christmas holiday?"

"Not yet, but I'll keep looking."

"I've been thinking about yesterday's accident." Alyson looked up from the report she was reading. "It occurred to me that the man in the wheelchair may have been involved."

"Involved how?"

"Randy said the safety bar on the chair had been working fine all day. He also said the lift itself had been running smoothly, and that he had been at his post at the bottom of the run. What about the top of the run? If the lift had to stop momentarily, isn't it possible someone at the top could have tampered with the lift and the chair?"

"I guess. The chair in question would have had to have been exactly at the top, though."

"Yeah, I guess it seems unlikely."

"I found something on Stacy King." Devon paused. "It says she was honorably discharged after being found innocent in a military court."

"Innocent of what?"

"I'm not sure. It just says that she was honorably discharged after serving three years of a four-year stint after a military court found her innocent of all charges."

"That's interesting."

"Very."

"So what are we thinking?" Alyson asked

"I have no idea. I'm sure this is relevant, though. I'm just not sure how."

"Keep looking. I think I'll heat up some of that chicken noodle soup I saw in the cupboard. Do you want anything?"

"No, not right now. Thanks anyway."

Alyson opened the soup, dumped it into a pan, and turned on the heat. She rummaged through the cupboard for some crackers. Getting sick was a total drag, but she was enjoying this time alone with Devon. She'd have to take Mac's advice and ask him about his future plans at some point. Maybe after they solved the crime and, hopefully, the bad guy was captured.

Alyson took her soup out to the living room. She opened the file and read a bunch of stuff they already knew. Todd Wallford had fallen to his death from chair 146 on Patty's run.

"Dev..."

"Yeah?"

"What was that code again? The one we found in Todd Wallford's wallet?"

"It was 16146138. Why."

"Look at this. The chair Todd fell from was number 146. What if the 146 in the code refers to the specific chair?"

"Maybe. I wonder what the other numbers mean."

Alyson searched the report for the other numbers. "It says he fell at approximately one forty. 138 could be the time he was supposed to get on the chair."

"You think he purposely got on that particular chair at that particular time?" Devon asked.

"Randy said Todd got to the front of the line, then talked to him while several others loaded. Maybe he was waiting for that specific chair to come around."

"Okay, why?"

"I don't know. I'm sure if he knew how his ride would end up he would have taken another chair."

"Maybe the killer promised him something," Devon speculated. "Or maybe he was blackmailing him, or it was some type of ransom situation. Whatever the reason, it appears Todd was instructed to take that particular chair on that particular run at that particular time."

"The 16 might be the run number. I think I saw a map somewhere around here. All the runs are numbered."

Devon looked around the room. "Here it is. Patty's run is number 16. I guess we figured out this clue. I'd better call my dad."

Alyson tossed the file aside and ate her tepid soup as Devon made the call.

"I had to leave a voice mail. Hopefully he'll call back soon. How's the soup?"

"Cold."

"I can make you some more."

"No, it's okay. If Todd Wallford did ride a particular chair on a particular run at a particular time maybe my idea about the disabled man isn't that far off. Suppose Bret somehow got the man to ride a particular chair at a specific time. He wanted to tamper with chair 146 and knew that when that chair was exactly at the top of the mountain chair 582 or whatever would be exactly at the bottom, so he arranged for someone who may or may not have actually been disabled, to ride that particular chair up the mountain just as 146 was headed down the mountain to pick up Wallford."

"As crazy as that sounds it makes sense. The only thing I don't get is why the killer went to so much trouble. I mean, slipping poison in a drink is a lot less work than arranging for such an intricate set of circumstances."

"Yeah," Alyson agreed, "it does seem odd that the deaths have all been so different. From a serial killer standpoint it would make more sense to kill everyone the same way. There must be a reason the killer is doing things the way he is. I mean, Mario was injured in an explosion. He happened to be off that day, so the killer had to arrange for Charlie to get food poisoning. Why not just wait until the next day, when Mario would be on duty?"

"Good point."

"Better yet, why not just slip some poison in his coffee? The timing and method of the deaths must have some sort of significance to the killer."

"Yeah, but what?" Devon asked.

"I have no idea. Other than the fact that he wanted the deaths to look like accidents."

"The more we research this the more complicated it gets."

"And we still don't have motives for the murders," Alyson pointed out. "I'm leaning toward Bret as the killer, but I can't imagine why he'd do it. I guess we should keep looking."

"Quite the task maker, aren't you?" Devon returned to the computer.

"I'd just really like to get this wrapped up. I can't help wondering if there are other intended victims. Maybe if we can get this figured out in time we can save a life."

"I'm not sure we can find the motive behind a psycho killer's actions on the Web," Devon said.

"At least we can try." Alyson sat quietly with her thoughts as Devon continued to work. If it weren't for the fact that there was a killer on the loose and she felt like crap she'd be having a really good time. The resort was absolutely fabulous.

"I think I found something," Devon said after several minutes.

"What?"

"A newspaper article. You'll want to take a look at this. There's a photo."

Alyson walked over to the computer and looked over Devon's shoulder. "Oh my God. I think we've found the murderer *and* the next victim."

Chapter 13

"'A military court in Washington, DC, ruled today that six of the seven defendants in the Kabul murders were innocent of all charges. The marine squad, made up of seven GIs, was dispatched to infiltrate a terrorist cell in the capital city of Kabul. The premises where the terrorists were believed to reside was ambushed and all occupants were killed. An investigation showed that the home was not occupied by armed terrorists but by an uninvolved family,'" Devon read.

"Oh God. No wonder Mario wanted to hide out. How awful. Couldn't they tell that the family was innocent?"

"There's more. 'An extensive investigation and interviews with all involved uncovered the fact that one member in the party was responsible for all the shooting, while the other six tried to stop him. The court ruled that Private Bret Robbins suffered a psychotic breakdown during the attack. He was transferred to a psychiatric facility upon deliverance of the verdict.'"

"So the other six were Mario, Stacy, Bruce, Martha, Todd, and…" Alyson asked.

"Someone named Mark Wallace."

"Do you think he's here?"

"I think we'd better find out. Get dressed; we'll see if Dawn at the front desk can tell us if he's registered. If we're lucky the slide kept him away."

Alyson threw on some clothes and returned to the living room, where Devon was leaving another message for his father.

"The others have the Expedition," Alyson pointed out.

"There's a two-seater snowmobile out back. We'll have to take that. Bundle up; it's bound to be a nippy ride and I don't want you getting any sicker than you already are."

Alyson pulled on her heaviest jacket and her hat, gloves, and snow boots. She wrapped a scarf around her neck for good measure and joined Devon outside.

The ride to the main lodge was indeed a chilly one. Devon had given her a helmet with a face shield, but she still could feel the cold air on her cheeks.

Devon pulled up in front of the lodge and hopped off. "I hope Dawn's here today. Someone who doesn't know us might not give us information about registered guests."

"Dawn," Alyson greeted her as they walked in. "I need to know if you have a Mark Wallace registered."

"I'll check. No, no Mark Wallace. We do have an employee named Mark Wallace, though."

"Where does he work?'

"He's on the avalanche crew. Just started a couple of months ago. You could check with security to see where he is right now. I heard they were going to clear the backside of the mountain today, so I'm betting he's there."

"This is pretty urgent. Can you call security for us to check?"

"Sure. Hang on."

"Clear the back side of the mountain?" Alyson whispered as Dawn called.

"If there's an avalanche danger they set off explosives to create a controlled avalanche. It lessens the potential for a real one."

"Security confirmed he's with the blast team," Dawn informed them.

"Do you have a map of where they are? Preferably a topographical one?" Devon asked.

"No, but I'll have Raina in security fax one over. Give me a few minutes."

"What good's a topographical map going to do us?" Alyson whispered. "Do you know how to read one?"

"Actually, I do. Plus I have a GPS back at the house. We'll pick it up on the way. Once we punch in the coordinates it should lead us right to him."

Alyson sneezed.

"Maybe you should wait at the house. I can go alone."

"No way. I'm going. I'll be fine."

"Okay, it's your fun case of pneumonia."

"I'm not going to get pneumonia. I just have a little cold."

"Here's the map." Dawn handed it to Devon. "I had Raina circle his probable location. Why do you want to see him so bad anyway?"

"You know all the weird stuff that's been happening lately?"

"'Nuff said. Good luck; there's some pretty steep terrain up there and the avalanche danger is rated as extreme today. Be careful."

"We will. Thanks again."

"Should we tell someone where we're going?" Alyson asked.

"I left a message for my dad and Dawn knows exactly where we're headed. Dad checks his messages like clockwork. At this point I'm not sure who else to trust."

"Good point."

"Let's get the GPS and head up the mountain. It's quite a ways. It'll probably take an hour or more to get there by snowmobile."

"That long? I'd better stock up on Kleenex."

The ride up the mountain was both long and dangerous. The fresh powder slowed the journey and made the trip more difficult. As the machine lumbered to plow through the soft snow, it threw up a trail that left both Devon and Alyson soaked to the skin.

"How much longer?" Alyson yelled.

"At least another half hour."

"I hope we're not too late."

"Me too. Maybe Bret's not even up there."

Alyson held on tight as they navigated the deep snow. It was too hard to be heard over the roar of the engine.

"Why do you think Bret killed all those people?" Alyson asked when they stopped so Devon could consult the map. "Do you think he felt betrayed when they testified against him?"

"Probably. Although Mario got him a job and covered for him when he flaked. You'd think that would count for something."

"People with psychological problems are capable of anything," Alyson said. "He expected to see terrorists in that house, so he saw them even when his eyes told him differently. Maybe he sees the rest of his squad as the enemy. Who knows how someone like that might think? I just hope we're not too late."

"I just hope we get there before the sun goes behind the mountain. I don't want to have to navigate this in the dark."

"Mac and the others are going to freak out when they get home and we're not there." Alyson realized they'd never make it back before they got home.

"I know. I didn't want to leave a note telling them where we were because then they'd really freak out. My dad will have to fill them in. I'm betting he's gotten my message by now and is right behind us."

"I hope so. Backup would be nice."

Devon tucked the map into his jacket and they continued on the journey. To say that it was cold would be putting it mildly. In fact, to say that it was freezing would be putting it mildly. Alyson was sure she was going to turn completely blue if they didn't arrive at their destination soon.

"I think I see something up ahead," Devon said. "A reflection of some type. Keep your eyes peeled. I think we're getting close."

"Any idea how we're going to stop Bret if he is up here? He has a closet full of explosives and we don't even have a slingshot, let alone a gun."

"Yeah, I thought of that. I'm hoping he won't be there and we can warn Mark before it's too late. If Bret's already there, chances are we're too late and we'll have to run."

"It looks like there's a platform of some type up ahead." Alyson pointed into the distance.

"Probably the launch pad from which they can set the explosion."

"It looks like there's someone walking around. Here's hoping its Mark and not Bret."

Devon drove closer, and Alyson hoped whoever was on the platform was so engrossed with their task they wouldn't notice them coming.

"There's someone on the mountain," Alyson said. "It looks like someone in snowshoes."

Suddenly there was a loud blast, and a wall of snow coursed down the mountain, taking the man on snowshoes with it.

"Oh, God. That guy just got buried alive," Alyson shouted.

"Hang on. I'm betting that was Mark, and Bret's going to notice us any minute."

Devon changed direction and headed into the trees, pushing the machine as fast as it would go. A bullet whizzed past them and ricocheted off a nearby tree. Devon headed deeper into the tree cover in an attempt to lose their tail. Several more bullets whizzed past before Devon managed to push far enough ahead to pull out of range.

"Are you okay?" he yelled.

"I'm fine."

Devon drove deeper and deeper into the forest until he was convinced they were no longer being followed.

"Do you think we're safe?" Alyson asked as Devon slowed down.

"I think so. It's almost dark. I'm betting he turned back. Probably figured the elements would take care of us."

"Will they? Take care of us? Do you have any idea where we are or how to get back?"

"No. I dropped the GPS when I was hauling through the trees. I suppose the village is down the mountain, but it's getting late, and even if we did happen to luck out and be in the general vicinity, we'd never make it before we froze to death. We need to find shelter."

"Shelter?" Alyson cried. "Shelter where? There's nothing as far as the eye can see but trees and snow. We're going to die, aren't we?"

"No, we're not going to die. Hang on; I'm going to climb to the top of that hill to see if I can get a sense of where we are. We still have the map. Maybe I can find a cave or something."

"Oh, great. Let's just bunk with Smokey."

"Alyson, you need to get a grip. We need to keep clear heads if we're going to get out of this."

Alyson took a deep breath and willed herself to shut out the hysteria that was threatening to take over. "You're right. I'm sorry. I'm hanging on. Let's go."

Devon drove to the top of the hill and got off the snowmobile. He sank to his waist in the fresh powder and slowly waded to the top of the summit, looking in all directions.

Alyson was shivering when he returned. "I think I saw a flash of some sort. Like a reflection. Let's head that way and see what we can find. Are you okay?"

"Cold," she stuttered. "It's gotten so cold."

"I know. Hang on. It won't be much longer. I think the reflection was from a metal roof. I remember someone mentioning that there were hunting cabins up here that are used in the summer."

Alyson prayed that Devon was right about the cabin. They'd never survive a night in the open.

She was shaking uncontrollably by the time they finally pulled up to the small hunting cabin. Devon picked her up and broke down the door.

The place was sparsely furnished, but there was a stone fireplace and a pile of wood. Devon set Alyson on a chair and started a fire. Then he searched the cabin for blankets. There was a double bed in the back room. Devon pulled off the mattress and set it on the floor in front of the fire. He piled all the blankets he could find on top of it and tucked everything in so any heat they generated would stay inside.

"Take off your clothes. They're soaking wet."

"Can't. Hands are frozen. Can't move."

Devon picked Alyson up and set her on the floor near the fire. He stripped off her wet hat, coat, and gloves. He pulled off her boots, followed by her jeans and sweater. When she was stripped down to her bra and underwear he wrapped her in the blankets and stripped off his own clothes down to his boxer shorts. He threw another log on the fire and climbed under the blankets with her.

"It's okay. You should be warm in a few minutes. Try to relax."

"So cold. Can't feel my legs or feet."

"It's okay. The feeling should return in a few minutes."

Devon tucked Alyson beneath him. Alyson continued to shake as he rubbed her limbs, she imagined, in an attempt to stimulate circulation.

"So how'd you like your first snowmobile ride?" Devon asked. "That's quite a machine. Pulled sixty even with both of us on it. I've been thinking about getting one, but I guess there's not much snow in Cutter's Cove. Maybe I'll get a Jet Ski this summer. It's probably a similar rush."

Alyson felt herself begin to warm.

"I hope Andi's dad isn't too upset about the dent we put in the side of the snowmobile when we sideswiped that tree." Devon continued to chatter on. "I heard Andi say he just got it this winter."

"Devon," Alyson whispered, "my legs. It feels like there are a million needles poking me."

"That's good. It means the circulation is coming back."

"It hurts."

Devon began rubbing her legs. Alyson started to cry as the pain increased.

"It's okay. Just a few more minutes, I promise."

Alyson balled up against the pain and Devon held her close. He whispered to her and kissed her neck. He promised the pain would be over soon, and when it was she'd start to feel warm.

Eventually, Alyson stopped crying and started to relax. She scooted closer to Devon and the warmth slowly returned to her limbs.

"Better?"

"I'm finally starting to feel warm."

"You know, I've been fantasizing for months about doing this. Maybe not in this exact situation."

"Devon..."

"Just kidding. Well, not really. But don't worry; I'm just trying to warm you up, nothing more."

"I can't help thinking about Mark Wallace. How awful to be buried alive. I think it's one of my worst fears, especially since the dreams I had last October, where I was buried in the cave-in."

"Mark was trained and experienced. Many avalanche victims survive. Maybe Mark's okay."

"Do you really believe that?"

"Sure. Why not?"

"You're such an optimist." Alyson began to relax as the rest of her body began to warm up.

"Hey, I said we'd be okay and we are. Sometimes optimism pays off. The power of positive thinking and all that."

"If you say so."

"I'm going to get up just for a minute," Devon informed Alyson.

"No."

"I want to put some more wood on the fire and drag those chairs over here so I can drape our clothes over them. We'll want them to be dry by tomorrow."

"Okay, but hurry back."

"I will."

Devon did as he'd said and then crawled back into the makeshift bed. He lay on his side and pulled Alyson's back against him. "Warm?"

"Yeah, it's nice."

"So what do you want to do tomorrow?" Devon asked.

"Not die trying to get back."

Alyson's breath was slow and steady. She felt herself become lethargic as the effects of the cold wore off.

Devon stroked her hair as she relaxed into him.

"It sounds like it's windy." Alyson closed her eyes.

"Yeah, it's starting to snow again."

"Oh, good. We're not only lost in the woods, we're lost in a blizzard."

"I doubt it's a blizzard. Just a little snow."

"Um." Alyson could feel herself drifting off.

"Alyson?"

"Um."

"I don't want you to go to sleep yet. Not until I'm sure you're okay. Maybe another hour or so."

"Okay. You'd better keep talking to me, though, or I'll fall asleep anyway."

"We could play Twenty Questions."

"You mean that thing where I ask you if it's bigger than a bread box?"

"Actually, I was thinking about the thing where I ask you what your favorite flower is and you ask me what my favorite color is. I've known you for four months. In some ways I feel like I know you better than I know anyone, and in others, it's like I don't know you at all."

"Yeah, that's me. I'm a mystery. You start. But nothing embarrassing."

"Okay. What's your favorite flower?"

"A dandelion," Alyson answered.

"Like those things you pick out of your lawn?"

"Yeah, those."

"Interesting choice."

"Not really. I like them because they're simple and free. They aren't confined to someone's perfectly maintained garden; they grow wild and happy wherever the wind takes them. They're hearty; you don't have to prune and fertilize them. And they're resilient; you can pluck them out and they keep coming back."

"Suddenly I have a new appreciation for dandelions. Okay, your turn."

"What's your middle name?" Alyson asked.

"I can't believe you went there."

"Come on. 'Fess up. Is it really bad?"

"Lovell."

"Lovell? Really?"

"It was my grandfather's name."

"Oh, that's sweet. I like that."

Devon shifted so that his arm was under Alyson's head and she was lying on his shoulder. He continued to gently stroke her hair as they talked.

"My turn. What's your middle name?"

Alyson froze. Middle name? Had they given her one? "I don't have one."

"Come on. I told you mine, now spill."

"No, really. Check my driver's license. No middle name."

"Okay, if you were going to give yourself a middle name, what would it be?"

Alyson thought for a minute. "Tiffany."

"Why Tiffany?"

"Tiffany was my best friend before I moved to Cutter's Cove. We met in playgroup when we were like three. Our moms were good friends, so we got to see each other a lot. She was funny and spontaneous, sensitive and compassionate. If I had a middle name I'd want it to have meaning. Your middle name is in honor of your grandfather; mine would be in honor of Tiff."

"You've never mentioned her before. Do you still keep in touch?"

"No. She died before I came to Cutter's Cove."

"Oh, Alyson. I'm sorry."

"Yeah, me too." Alyson lay quiet for a minute, remembering Tiffany's laugh and smile. She'd make some big game out of being trapped in the middle of nowhere in a snowstorm.

"Favorite childhood memory," she finally said.

"Childhood memory?"

"Yeah, from when you were younger and smaller than you are now."

"Wow, that's a hard one. I guess it would be the summer my dad and mom and Eli and I all went camping. We set up a tent right near the lake and every night we'd build a fire and sing campfire songs. My dad taught me how to fish that summer. And best of all, no electricity so no computers. When we were at home Dad tended to get caught up in projects and lose track of time. But that summer we had his undivided attention."

"That sounds nice. My family never went camping; my parents tended to vacation at five-star resorts. That was nice too, but camping sounds like fun."

"I know your mom and she doesn't strike me as the five-star resort type," Devon said.

"She's not anymore. That was a different life. Now she'd probably really enjoy the camping thing; that is, if there were plumbing and mattresses. Maybe RV camping would be more her style."

"Okay, let's see.... What's your greatest fear?" Devon asked.

Having the Bonatello brothers find me. "Right now I'm thinking dying in this cabin, but actually I guess it would have to be losing someone I love. I've lost enough people in my life; the ones I have now I'd like to keep."

"We're not going to die, you know. I'll get us out of here."

"I know. I'm just being weak and pathetic, which, by the way, I hate, so let's move on. Let's see, what should I ask you? I know: who was your first kiss?"

"Trina Longsville in the first grade. She was quite the cutie. I paid her a nickel to kiss me behind the school."

"You paid her?"

"Hey, a man's gotta do what a man's gotta do. She was the cutest girl in my class and I really wanted to kiss her."

"Have you paid anyone else since?"

"That's another question and it's not your turn." Devon's hand drifted down her arm. Tiny pinpricks followed his fingers. "What's something you've never done that you've always wanted to do?"

"Mac, Trevor, and I cut down and decorated my Christmas tree this year. Up until a couple of weeks ago that probably would have been my answer. My parents always had a decorating service do ours. It was fun to decorate our tree with ornaments I picked out. I guess that doesn't really answer your question, though. I guess my answer would have to be to fall in love. I used to watch all those old Fred Astaire and Ginger Rogers movies with my aunt when I was a kid. You know the ones, where some guy would sing and dance his way into her heart. They were so romantic. I used to fantasize about waltzing around some huge ballroom with my own handsome prince."

"And now? Do you still fantasize about a prince who will sing and dance into your heart?"

"No. I guess my notions of the perfect guy have changed. Seriously, if some guy walked up to me and broke into song I'd probably call the cops. Okay, my question. When you were a little boy what did you want to be when you grew up?"

"Honestly, the same thing I want to be now—a software developer like my dad. I know most little boys want to be firefighters or doctors, but I've always been fascinated by computers."

"Well, it looks like you'll get your dream. You've been accepted into a great college."

"Yeah, looks like. Okay, my turn. If singing and dancing aren't the primary attributes you're looking for in a guy, what are?"

"I guess someone who's always there for me. Who's strong and independent but secure enough to let me be strong and independent; someone who knows me and accepts me for who I am, flaws and all. Someone who's is more interested in supporting me than coddling and protecting me."

"Sounds like you've thought about this."

"Not really. I just know what I want. I can't believe how tired I am."

"It's probably okay to go to sleep now. Your brain doesn't seem to be scrambled."

"Dev..."

"Huh?"

"Thanks. For today; for basically saving my life."

"No need to thank me. We were partners in this little adventure, however ill-advised it might have been. Partners always look out for each other."

"Well, thanks anyway."

Devon kissed Alyson on the head. "Get some sleep. Tomorrow's going to be a long day. You'll need your energy."

Alyson felt herself drifting off to that place where dreams become reality and the world melts away. She felt herself being drawn toward a point in the distance, a point where the darkness was bathed in light.

"Tiffany?"

"Hey, Amanda."

"What are you doing here?"

"I have no idea. It's your dream. Why'd you bring me here?"

"I didn't bring you here. At least I don't think I did. I was talking to Devon and then, all of the sudden, here you were. I'm glad to see you, though."

"Me too. That Devon is quite a hunk. Is he your boyfriend?"

"Sort of. I guess. Honestly, I'm not sure."

"How can you not be sure?"

"It's complicated."

"Does he know who you really are?"

"No. I guess that's part of the problem."

"So tell him."

"I can't. You know I can't."

"Mac knows. Do you trust Mac more than you trust Devon?"

"No, it's not that. Mac found out on her own. I couldn't help that."

"That's not really true. Mac found the picture, but you didn't have to tell her. You could have lied. It would have been easy to do it. You've been lying for so long it's become part of who you are."

"I don't want it to be. Maybe that's why I couldn't lie to Mac. I needed for someone to know."

"So tell Devon."

"I wish I could, but I can't."

"Are you afraid that he'll look at you differently? That if you show him your true face he won't like what he sees?"

"Maybe. I don't know; you're confusing me."

"You have to make a choice. He loves you. You can't let him love you if he doesn't even know who you are."

"I guess I can't."

Chapter 14

Alyson woke up the next morning alone in the makeshift bed. She slowly opened her eyes. She could hear Devon in the kitchen. She tried to sit up, but her head started spinning. She lay back down and willed the world to come into focus.

"Look what I found." Devon walked into the room completely dressed in the clothes he'd worn the day before. He handed her a cup with black liquid. "It's instant but still caffeinated."

Alyson wrapped the blanket more tightly around her half-naked body and took the cup.

"You look a little pale. Are you feeling okay?" Devon asked.

"Not really. I feel a little funky."

Devon put his palm against her forehead. "You feel warm. I'm afraid yesterday's snow bath didn't help much. There are a few canned goods in the kitchen. Feel like eating something?"

"Sure. I'll just get dressed, then meet you in there."

"It's cold in the other room. You wait in here and I'll bring the food." Devon walked back the way he'd come.

Alyson got up and dressed in the clothes that had dried overnight. She took several long sips of her coffee as she stood at the window and watched the snow.

"We're in luck." Devon walked into the room carrying a frying pan and a can of something. "Among the other things I found a can of Spam."

"Spam?"

"Mechanically separated meat parts reformed into a handy little cube. A staple for camping. Surely you've tried it."

"No, I'm afraid I haven't."

"Then you're in for a real treat. We'll slice it thin, then fry it over the fire. I found a can of beans to go with it. Believe me, you haven't lived until you've had Spam and beans for breakfast."

"Sounds good." Alyson sat down on one of the rickety wooden chairs that surrounded the wooden dining table. "It's snowing pretty hard again. Do you think we'll be able to find our way back?"

"I've been thinking about that." Devon stirred the beans. "Between the weather, your fever, and our complete lack of knowing where we are, I think we should wait it out a day. My dad and the others know we're missing, they know where we were headed, and I'm betting Andi's dad and the security team know about this cabin. My bet is that they'll come looking for us."

"What if Bret comes looking for us first?"

Devon set a plate of beans and Spam in front of Alyson. "I'm hoping he assumes we perished in the elements, but even if he's still out there, our chances of coming out of this alive seem greater if we stay put than if we wander out into a storm."

"But what if he does show up?" Alyson took a small forkful of beans. "Do we just sit here and let him shoot us? Shouldn't we have a plan?"

"Let's eat and then we can look around to see if there's anything we can use as a weapon. We'll figure out how to deal with him before he gets here."

"Okay," she said. "You were right. This Spam is really good. I'll have to pick some up when I get home."

"Spam is more of a frying-over-a-campfire kind of product," Devon informed Alyson. "I doubt you'd like it near as much if you prepared it in your own kitchen. It's more of a theme meat."

"I see."

"You seemed pretty restless last night. Did you sleep okay?"

"I kept having these funky dreams."

"I guess that's to be expected under the circumstances."

"Yeah, I guess. Dev..."

"Yeah?"

"Do you think it's important for two people who care about each other to know everything about each other?"

"I'm not sure it's possible to know everything about another person, but yeah, I guess it's important that two people in a relationship know each other pretty well. Hence last night's game. Before that I would have wasted my money buying you roses for Valentine's Day. Now I know I just need to pick dandelions out of the lawn."

"The lawn's dormant in February. There won't be any dandelions till spring."

"I guess I'll have to have some imported from the south."

Alyson laughed. "Seems like a lot of trouble for a flower."

"Yeah, but not for a girl."

Alyson felt her heart begin to melt. She thought of Tiffany's words. She knew she was going to have to make up her mind about Devon before things went any further.

Alyson and Devon finished eating, then took an inventory of the cabin. There were enough canned goods to last almost a week if need be, and plenty of firewood stacked up under a tarp on the deck behind the cabin. Although there was no running water, there was loads of fresh snow, which Devon had melted to make the coffee that morning.

"I don't suppose you happened to run across any guns, did you?" Alyson asked.

"'Fraid not."

"Maybe a bow and arrow? Sharp knife? Slingshot?"

"It looks like whoever uses this cabin in the summer took his weapons with him. I did find a knife, though, and some rope."

"We're going to have to get pretty close to use either of those."

"I also found a couple of fishing poles, a tackle box, and several animal traps."

"I'd feel a lot better if we had a couple of guns. Big guns; maybe a rocket launcher."

"I have an idea." Devon sat down at the table. "The deck out back is about a foot off the ground. Just enough for us to slide under. If we spread the wood out over the surface of the deck someone standing on it wouldn't be able to see through the cracks."

"You think we should hide under the deck if he comes? We'd be trapped."

"The idea is to trap him. Here's the plan."

Devon spent the next fifteen minutes outlining what they'd do. They would use the snowmobile to make fresh tracks out back, leading away from the cabin. They would double back and stash the snowmobile in the back bedroom and cover it with sheets. Hopefully, Bret wouldn't think to look under them. At the end of the snowmobile path, they'd create a footpath into the trees. They would carefully backtrack, so the path would appear to head in just one direction. Along the footpath they'd bury the animal traps he'd found. Hopefully Bret would find his way into one of them.

"So now we just wait?" Alyson asked.

"We wait and hope the rescue team gets here before Bret does. In the meantime, I found some cards in one of the kitchen drawers. I'm thinking strip poker."

"How about gin rummy. For points, not pants."

"Rummy it is."

"This waiting is starting to get to me." Alyson discarded a card and picked up another one later that afternoon. "I keep thinking I hear things."

"If anyone shows up on a snowmobile we'll hear them long before they get here. The sightline down the mountains is pretty good from here. If Bret shows up we'll have at least several minutes' warning."

Alyson bit her lip as she rearranged her cards and tried to figure out a strategy. "I bet Mac and the others are going crazy right about now. I know I would be if it was one of them missing."

"I wish there was a way to let them know we're all right, but I think all we can do is wait and hope someone finds us."

"It looks like it stopped snowing. Maybe we should just head down the mountain and hope for the best."

"It's afternoon. We only have a few hours of daylight. If it's clear tomorrow and no one has found us yet, maybe we'll try then. I guess we could always follow our tracks back here if we get lost."

Alyson threw away her king and prayed for a two. "I've been thinking a lot about the murders since we've been here. I have to say I still don't get it. Even if Bret felt he had motive to kill these particular people, why use so many different methods to achieve his objective? There has to have been a reason."

Devon discarded a four and picked up an eight. "We'll probably never know.

Mario was injured in an explosion. Bruce Long froze to death. Stacy King was poisoned. Todd Wallford fell to his death. Martha Strom was burned to death. Mark Wallace was buried alive. All different causes of death but no common variable that I can see."

"It's not even like there was an increasing level of violence with each attack. Mario's accident was pretty violent, but Bruce and Stacy's were fairly nonviolent by comparison."

"I guess only Brett knows why he did what he did the way he did it."

"Gin." Alyson lay her cards on the table. "I win again."

"What are you, some kind of a card shark? That's seven games in a row. Are you cheating?"

"Wouldn't you like to know?"

"Seriously..."

"No, I'm not cheating. You appear to be a very conservative player. I've watched you. You get your initial hand, come up with a strategy, and stick with it. Do you know you almost never rearrange your cards once you initially arrange them? Sometimes you have to throw away your original plan, throw caution to the winds, and go for something totally different."

"You are a card shark. When we get out of here we're going to Vegas."

Alyson shuffled the deck and dealt the cards. "I've been meaning to ask you what your plans are for after the trip. I mean other than Vegas. You've basically graduated."

"Actually, I'm not sure yet. I was offered an internship with a top software company."

"Dev, that's great. Congratulations."

"It's in Los Angeles. I haven't definitely decided to take it, though."

"Why wouldn't you take it? It sounds like exactly the kind of thing that can help you with your career. Besides, you love LA."

"I know. It's just that I'll be going to college in the fall and I guess I thought I'd have a little more time to spend with…" Devon paused, "my friends before I had to go. If I take the internship I'll be gone the rest of the winter and most of the summer."

"Devon, you aren't seriously thinking about turning it down, are you? It's such a great opportunity."

"I know. It's just that it kind of came out of the blue. I wasn't planning for it. I got an e-mail last week offering it to me.

I'd have to start right after the New Year. It just seemed kind of sudden."

"Sometimes you have to be spontaneous and go for what you really want. Life's about choices. Every day we're all faced with choices, some big and some small. I think when we look back on our lives we'll see that there were several key junctures, major choices that defined who we became. I've always believed that it's the opportunities we say yes to that truly define us. You've wanted to be a software developer your whole life. You need to go for the things that are important to you. Take a risk; go all in."

"Yeah, I guess. I just thought maybe … forget it. Alyson, do you …"

"Do you hear something?" Alyson interrupted.

Devon listened. "Sounds like a snowmobile." He wandered over to the window. "Someone's coming. It looks like a single rider. A rescue team would be in a group."

"It's Bret."

"Probably. Bundle up, then get under the deck. I'll be there in a minute."

"But…"

"Just do it. Crawl as far under as you can. Get comfortable, then lay very still."

Alyson pulled on her boots, hat, gloves, and jacket. She took one of the blankets to lay on, then got on her belly and crawled under the deck. She could feel the two-by-fours used to support the decking rub against her back as she crawled. She hoped there weren't spiders—or worse, snakes—hibernating under the deck. When she crawled in as far as she could, she spread out the blanket and waited.

Several minutes later Devon crawled in behind her. "It's Bret all right," he whispered. "Whatever you do, don't make a sound."

Alyson nodded and willed her breathing to slow. She was sure Bret would be able to hear her heart beating. Devon held her hand as they waited for Bret to find his way out back.

Alyson could hear Bret moving around inside. He was calling to them. As if they'd come, even if they were hiding in a closet or under a bed. Eventually, he made his way onto the back deck.

"You guys out here? I just want to talk. Really, you can come out."

Alyson held her breath and prayed Bret wouldn't find them. She closed her eyes and willed herself not to panic. Her instinct was to run, not passively wait to be found.

Bret walked a short way down the snowmobile path, then returned inside through the back door. Alyson heard him leave through the front door and start his snowmobile. Several seconds later, he sped around the side of the house and down the path.

"What now?" Alyson whispered.

"We wait. It won't take him more than ten or fifteen minutes to follow our track to the end. If we don't catch him in one of the traps he'll probably be back this way."

"And if we do catch him? Then what?"

"I guess we'll tie him up and wait for the cavalry."

"He probably has a gun. Chances are he'll shoot us before we can even get close to him. Besides, how do we open the trap?"

"There's a tool. We'll get him to throw his gun away before we help him."

"How are we even going to get close enough to talk to him? It's too bad the hunter didn't leave behind bulletproof vests or something."

"We'll figure something out." Devon squeezed her hand. "Once we trap him we'll have the upper hand."

"I hope so. I think I feel something crawling up my leg." Alyson started to squirm around.

"It's probably just your imagination. Lay still."

"I have a black widow, or maybe even a tarantula, crawling up my leg and you tell me to lay still?"

"It's too cold for either of those. Do you hear something?"

"A snowmobile. Darn; our trap must not have worked."

"No, it sounds like it's coming from down the hill behind us. Wait here." Devon started to crawl out.

"Devon, wait. What if he just circled around and is coming back?"

"I doubt he would have had time to do that. I'll check it out, then come right back. Now be quiet."

Devon crawled out from under the deck and went in through the cabin. Alyson tried to listen, but she couldn't hear anything except her own heartbeat. Eventually the sound of snowmobiles became louder. She could definitely hear several. It sounded like they were coming from both sides.

Where was Devon? He'd said he'd be right back. Right back was maybe a minute, two at the most. He'd been gone at least five. Alyson heard footsteps on the deck.

"Dev?" she called.

"Well, well, well. What do we have here?" Bret was looking under the deck. "Come on out of there and maybe I won't shoot you."

"I can't; I'm stuck." *Come on, Dev. Where are you?*

"I doubt that. Now be a good girl and come on out. I can shoot you from here, you know. The bullets from this gun will travel right through the decking and into your pretty little head."

"Okay, I'm coming."

Alyson crawled out and Bret grabbed her.

"Where's your boyfriend?"

"He's not here. He went for help. I'm sure he'll be back any minute with the police."

"Why don't I believe you? Maybe because there are no snowmobile tracks going down the hill toward the village. Your little diversion was inspired, though. I especially liked the use of the traps. If I hadn't been ex-military and trained to watch where I step, you might have got me. Now where's lover boy?" Bret shoved the gun in her back.

"I don't know. Really. He told me to hide, that he was going for help."

"You kids are really starting to grate my hide. Mark was my last one. If you hadn't stuck your nose in where it didn't belong I'd be on my way out of the country by now."

"How? The roads are closed."

"Didn't you hear? They opened them. After I finish off you and lover boy I'm outta here. Heard Mexico's nice this time of year, and a whole lot warmer. Then again, maybe I'll take you along. I haven't had a pretty young thing to warm my bed in quite a while."

"Thanks, but I'd rather die. Why'd you do it? Why'd you kill all your friends? They served in the war with you. Mario got you a job when you got out. They were like family and you killed them."

"They used me. They set me up and made me the scapegoat. We were all in it together, but I was the only one to end up in some damn psychiatric hospital for five years."

"The article I read said you were the only one to fire on the family."

"I was following orders. I couldn't help it if the higher-ups got the wrong intel. Someone tells me to shoot, I shoot. If the others were so innocent why didn't any of them try to stop me? They stood by and watched me do all the dirty work, and then they turned on me to save their own hides."

"I guess I see your point. Still, killing them seems a bit extreme."

"Do you have any idea how they treat you in those psycho wards? Killing them was nothing compared to what I had to endure all those years. I was a good soldier with a promising future, but they took it all away from me. All they had to do was testify that the people had guns, that they were aggressive and we acted in self-defense. All they had to do was back me up and we all would have gotten out of there with honorable discharges. We were a team; they should have had my back. Instead, they deserted me. They all went home and left me to waste away in that pit of a facility. Marines don't leave team members behind. It's the first rule of combat. They violated that rule. They deserved to die."

"I'm sorry."

"Enough of the sweet talk. Get inside. Let's see if we can't find your boyfriend. I'm really anxious to tie up my loose ends and get started south."

Alyson walked inside with the gun to her back. Where was Devon? He must have seen what was happening. There weren't a lot of places to hide. Bret was sure to find him.

Suddenly a log came flying through the air and hit Bret in the head. Bret stumbled and Devon hit him from behind, knocking the gun out of his hand. Alyson grabbed the gun while Devon and Bret wrestled on the floor. Alyson aimed the gun in the air and pulled the trigger.

Both men stopped fighting when the ceiling exploded above them.

"Get up and put your hands behind your back," Alyson demanded.

"You may as well kill me 'cause there's no way I'm going quietly." Bret got up and started toward Alyson. She pulled the trigger and he crumpled to the floor.

Devon rushed over and took the gun from Alyson's shaking hand. "Are you okay?"

"Yeah. Is he dead?"

Devon felt for a pulse. "No, he's alive. The security patrol is on the way up the hill. I saw them earlier. They should be here any minute."

"Good. I'm feeling a little dizzy. I think I should sit down. Maybe you should tie him up or something."

"Yeah, maybe I should."

Chapter 15

The security patrol showed up ten minutes later. They applied emergency treatment to Bret's wound and called for a chopper to evacuate him. Alyson and Devon caught a ride with the chopper back to the resort.

"Oh my God, I was so worried." Mac was strangling Alyson as she cried into her hair. "You should never have gone off on your own. You could have been killed. What were you thinking?"

"It's okay. I'm fine. We're both fine."

"I thought you were dead. Do you have any idea how it feels to wonder if your best friend is dead or alive?"

"Actually, I do. I'm sorry I put you through all that."

Trevor grabbed Alyson and hugged her until it felt like her ribs were going to break. "I am so going to kill you. What were you thinking? You could have died up there on that mountain."

"Me dead? Nah. You know me; I'm the resilient type. It takes a lot more than one psycho killer to put me in the ground. Besides, I had Devon. He was great. Where is he anyway?"

"I don't know. I saw him come in, but then he went upstairs. I haven't seen him since."

Alyson took Mac's hand in one of hers and Trevor's in the other. "I'm truly sorry for what I put you through. I guess we didn't think everything through. When we found out about Mark our only thought was to try to warn him before it was too late. I guess the whole thing was for nothing, though."

"No, you did save his life," Mac informed her. "Eli's dad got Devon's message. The security team got to him before he died. He's in the hospital, but he's going to be fine."

"You're kidding. He lived through that? I saw the mountain of snow. I don't see how anyone could have survived that."

"Mark's a professional. He knew what to do. By the time the security team got to him he had already managed to send a ski pole through to the surface. They actually got him out pretty fast."

"You have no idea how happy I am to hear that. Somehow knowing that our actions helped Mark makes me feel a whole lot better about the rest. We should tell Devon."

"I'll get him," Trevor volunteered.

Devon walked downstairs a few minutes later with his suitcase in his hand.

"Are you going somewhere?" Eli asked.

"I decided to take that internship I've been thinking about. The chopper pilot said he'd give me a ride to the airport. I decided to take his offer. I still need to pack and arrange for temporary housing."

"Are you sure?" Eli asked. "The New Year's Eve party is tonight. I thought you were looking forward to going."

"I was, but I decided this was more important. There will be other parties; this internship is important for my career. By the way, I heard about Mark. I'm really glad he's okay. I'm glad we all are."

"Okay. I guess we'll hook up when we get back."

"Yeah. We'll hook up."

Devon shook Trevor and Eli's hands, he gave Andi and Mac a hug, and then kissed Alyson on the top of the head. The chopper was waiting for him at the launch pad. Trevor and Eli volunteered to drive him over to it. Andi decided to go along, then have them drop her at home on their way back.

Trevor and Eli went outside, leaving Mac and Alyson alone.

"Do you want to talk about it?" Mac sat down on the sofa next to Alyson.

"Talk about what?"

"You and Devon. Something must have happened for him to just up and leave like that. I mean, we're all leaving in a few days and all of a sudden there's all this urgency to get back."

"Nothing happened."

"Alyson, you're my best friend. I'm your best friend. You can tell me."

"Things just got intense while we were gone."

"Of course they got intense. Some psycho lunatic tried to kill you."

"That's not what I mean. When we were at the cabin things got ... intimate."

"Oh."

"Not that kind of intimate. More like emotionally intimate. We talked about a lot of things that we'd never talked about before. Personal things about who we were and where we came from and what we wanted out of life. Stuff like that."

"You told him about Amanda?" Mac asked.

"No. I couldn't. That's the problem; here we were in this intimate situation, sharing our dreams and memories, and I couldn't tell him anything real about myself. I think he's falling in love with me. There were things he said that kind of led to that conclusion."

"Do you love him back?"

"I don't know. Maybe if I could. But I can't. We've discussed this before; I can never tell him who I am."

"Devon seems pretty trustworthy."

"It's not that. By telling him I'd be putting him in danger. I never should have told you. I worry every day that your knowledge of my past will someday come back to bite you. I could never live with myself if anything happened to any of you."

"So you broke up with him?"

"Not exactly. He told me about the internship he was considering and I sort of pushed him into it. I have a feeling he was thinking about turning it down because of us. I couldn't let him do that."

"Yeah, I guess not. Can I do anything?"

"Honestly, I think I just need some sleep."

"Okay. I'll be in the kitchen if you need me."

Alyson lay back on the couch and pulled the hand-quilted comforter over her. She let a single tear escape as she mourned what she could have had with Devon if things were different. As she dropped off to sleep she willed herself to dream about a happier time, when her life would once again be her own and she no

longer had to hide from who she really
was.

Kathi Daley lives with her husband, kids, grandkids, and Bernese mountain dogs in beautiful Lake Tahoe. When she isn't writing, she likes to read (preferably at the beach or by the fire), cook (preferably something with chocolate or cheese), and garden (planting and planning, not weeding). She also enjoys spending time on the water when she's not hiking, biking, or snowshoeing the miles of desolate trails surrounding her home.

Kathi uses the mountain setting in which she lives, along with the animals (wild and domestic) that share her home, as inspiration for her cozy mysteries.

Stay up-to-date with her newsletter, *The Daley Weekly*. There's a link to sign up on both her Facebook page and her website, or you can access the sign-in sheet at: http://eepurl.com/NRPDf

Visit Kathi:
Facebook at Kathi Daley Books,
www.facebook.com/kathidaleybooks

Kathi Daley Teen –
www.facebook.com/kathidaleyteen

Kathi Daley Books Group Page –
https://www.facebook.com/groups/
569578823146850/

Kathi Daley Books Birthday Club- get a
book on your birthday -
https://www.facebook.com/groups/
1040638412628912/

Kathi Daley Recipe Exchange -
https://www.facebook.com/groups/
752806778126428/

Webpage - www.kathidaley.com

E-mail - kathidaley@kathidaley.com

Recipe Submission E-mail –
kathidaleyrecipes@kathidaley.com

Goodreads:
https://www.goodreads.com/author/
show/7278377.Kathi_Daley

Twitter at Kathi Daley@kathidaley -
https://twitter.com/kathidaley

Pinterest -
http://www.pinterest.com/kathidale
y/

50284566R00134

Made in the USA
Charleston, SC
20 December 2015